W9-CNL-737

ASYLUM PIECE

Also available from Michael Kesend Publishing, Ltd.
By Anna Kavan

SLEEP HAS HIS HOUSE

ASYLUM PIECE

and Other Stories

by

ANNA KAVAN

Windsor Public Library

Michael Kesend Publishing, Ltd.

Copyright © by Anna Kavan 1940
                © by Rhys Davies and R.B. Marriott 1972

All rights reserved under International and Pan-American
Copyright Conventions. Published in the United States by
Michael Kesend Publishing, Ltd. 1025 Fifth Avenue, New York,
N.Y. 10028. Originally published in Great Britain by Peter
Owen Limited.

Library of Congress Cataloging in Publication Data
Edmonds, Helen Woods
    Asylum piece and other stories.
    Contents: The birthmark. — Going up in the world. — The
enemy, and other stories.
    I. Title
PZ3.E241As 1980 (PR6009.D63) 823'.912 79-28536
ISBN 0-935576-02-9

Designed by Peter McKenzie

Manufactured in the United States of America

BUDIMIR MEMORIAL LIBRARY

Contents

PREFACE

I was introduced to Anna Kavan and to her work in 1956 by a mutual friend, Diana Johns, who ran a bookshop which Anna frequented. This was shortly after publication of her novel *A Scarcity of Love*. Following the book boom of the late 'forties Anna had found in increasingly difficult to find publishers for her work, and her reputation, which had seemed secure, was declining. Lacking any offers for *A Scarcity of Love*, she partly subsidized its publication; but the publisher, an acquaintance of hers on the periphery of book publishing, lacked distribution facilities and failed to pay his printer. His subsequent bankruptcy prevented even a moderate circulation of the book—which my firm successfully reissued in 1971.

Anna, who was then living in a beautiful house which she had converted in Peel Street, Kensington, was in the throes of litigation with the builders: Showing me their slovenly work, she explained that she was obliged to convert houses to supplement the small income bequeathed to her by her wealthy mother. She told me that she was a compulsive writer and was only happy when writing. During this first visit of mine, she handed me the manuscript of a new novel, *Eagles' Nest*. We published this book in 1957 and, despite poor sales, followed it with a volume of stories, *A Bright Green Field*, the next year.

Anna Kavan was a lonely person, aloof with strangers, who relaxed only among a few intimate friends. Her regular visitors included the writer Rhys Davies and a doctor called Blut. Sometimes I visited her for drinks or dinner. She was an excellent hostess and a good cook. It was some time before I realized that she was an incurable heroin addict; this was not evident either in her behavior or in her smart appearance.

In about 1960 she completed a short novel which was good, but it seemed to me to be too short to make a book and at that time my firm's imprint was not well enough established to allow deviation from the more conventional formats. Of course I gave her my reasons for rejecting it. A year or so later I reapproached her about the novella, since I now felt confident to publish it, only to be told that she had destroyed it after my rejection. It was around this time that she sold the Peel Street house and had built to her design another one nearby, which remained her home until her death. Occasionally she augmented her income by selling personal treasures, such as her Graham Sutherland painting, which saddened her. From time to time, she sent me stories—some of them were brilliant, whilst others fell below the general high standard she had set herself. Like many other writers, Anna was a bad judge of her own work. I thought it important that only her best writing should be published. Another novel appeared under the Scorpion Press imprint in the 'sixties.

In 1967 I agreed to publish *Ice*, after some revisions were made. This and some of her later stories which *Encounter* published were verging on science-fiction. When I remarked on this she replied: 'That's the way I see the world now.' The publication of *Ice* and of several stories in magazines helped restore her reputation to some extent. The editors of *Encounter* assumed that the stories I had sent them were by a talented new writer, and when her identity was revealed they commented: 'Is it *the* Anna Kavan? We though she was dead!' Anna kept her age a closely guarded secret. After the publication of *Ice*, having heard of her sale of the Sutherland, I suggested she might be eligible for an Arts Council grant. Her surprising reluctance to respond to my suggestion was later explained to me by Rhys Davies: she refused to divulge her date of birth on the application form.

I had known for some time that Anna was unwell but without appreciating the seriousness of her illness. Early in December 1968 my wife and I invited her to a housewarming party, and she said she hoped to come—which rather surprised me, since as a rule she avoided social gatherings of this kind. Shortly after the party the police telephoned me, having found our invitation card in her house, which they had broken into at the request of Rhys Davies. She had died on the evenings of our party.

The morning of her funeral I received the news that Doubleday, her American publishers of the 'forties, had bought *Ice*.

For the most part neglected in her lifetime, Anna Kavan's posthumous reputation is growing. French, Dutch, Italian, Japanese, Swedish, Danish, Portuguese and Spanish editions of her work have been published; translations of her work; stories by her have appeared in leading British, American and

Dutch magazines; her books are becoming something of a cult. I believe this edition of one of her early books, *Asylum Piece*, to be long overdue. First published in England in 1940, it was highly praised by critics and in a long commendatory review of it in the *Sunday Times* Sir Desmond MacCarthy wrote: "There is a beauty about these stories which has nothing to do with their pathological interest, and is the result of art. Two or three, if signed by a famous name, might rank among the story-teller's memorable achievements. There is beauty in the stillness of the author's ultimate despair.'

It is sad that writers whose vision transcends that of their contemporaries often remain unappreciated in their own lifetime.

Peter Owen
Peter Owen Ltd.

ASYLUM PIECE

The Birthmark

THE BIRTHMARK

WHEN I was fourteen my father's health made it necessary for him to go abroad for a year. It was decided that my mother should accompany him, our home was temporarily closed, and I was sent to a small boarding school in the country.

At this school I got to know a girl called H. I purposely use the words 'got to know' in preference to the words 'made friends with,' because, although I was acutely conscious of her all the time, I remained there, no actual friendship developed between us.

It was at supper time on my first day at the school that H first caught my attention. I was sitting beside another new girl at the long table, feeling strange and subdued and a little homesick in this noisy environment so different from the enclosed, intimate atmosphere in which the whole of my life had been passed up to that day. I looked at the young faces of these still unknown companions, some of whom were to become friends, some enemies. One face among them all held my eyes with compelling attraction.

H was sitting on the opposite side of the table, almost immediately facing me. In the midst of so many brown heads her fairness alone was arresting. It was an autumn evening, misty and cold, and the room was not too well lighted. I had the impression that what light there was in the dining hall clustered around her, reviving and renewing itself as it played upon her fair hair. In looking back I think that she must have been beautiful; yet the detailed picture of her obstinately eludes me, I can recall only an impression of a face unique, neither gay nor melancholy, but endued with a peculiar quality of apartness, the look of a person dedicated to some accepted destiny. Perhaps these phrases sound out of place in connection with a schoolgirl who was only a few months older than I; and naturally I did not think of her in that way at the time. It is the accumulated rather than the momentary impression which I want to convey. Just then I saw only a fair girl, slightly my senior, who, catching my eyes upon her and doubtless thinking that I might be in need of encouragement, smiled at me across the table.

I remember that I looked back at her with some envy. It seemed to me then that she must possess everything that I, as a newcomer, lacked — success, popularity, an established place in the school world. Afterwards I found out that this was not quite the case. A curious shade seemed to dim all H's activities. I came to look upon this shadow, so hard to describe in words, as being on some way the complement of her rare outward brilliance.

How can I convey the strange sense of nullification that accompanied her? Although she was not unpopular, she had no intimate friends; and although she was in the first rank both as regards work and sport, some inevitable accidental happening always debarred her from supreme achievement. This fate she seemed to accept without question: almost, one would have thought, without being aware of it. I never heard her complain of the bad luck which so consistently robbed her of every prize.

And yet she was certainly neither indifferent nor unaware.

I recall very clearly an occasion towards the end of my time at school. In one of the corridors was a baize-covered board to which, among other notices, was fastened a large sheet of paper bearing our names and the number of marks which each of us received every week. H was standing in front of this list, quite alone, looking at it with an expression that I did not understand, an expression not of resentment, not of regret, but, so it seemed to me, of resignation combined with dread. Seeing that look on her face I was overcome by a wave of passionate and inexplicable compassion; an emotion so profound, so apparently unjustified by the circumstances, that I was astonished to feel tears in my eyes.

'Let me help you . . . Let me do something,' I heard myself imploring, inarticulate as though my own fate were at stake.

Instead of answering me, H rolled up one of her sleeves and silently pointed to a blemish on her upper arm. It was a birthmark, faint as if traced in faded ink, which at first sight seemed to be no more than a little web of veins under the skin. But as I examined it more closely I saw that it resembled a medallion, a miniature design, a circle armed with sharp points and enclosing a tiny shape very soft and tender — perhaps a rose.

'Have you ever seen that anywhere else?' she asked me; and it crossed my mind that she hoped that I too bore a similar mark.

Was it disappointment, embarrassment or despair that appeared on her face as I reluctantly shook my head? I only know that she hurried out of the corridor and that for the rest of the time I was at school she seemed to avoid me and that we were never alone together again.

The years passed, and though I heard nothing about H, I never really forgot her. Every now and then, once or twice a year, when I was in a train, or waiting for an appointment, or getting dressed in the morning, the thought of her would come to me, together with a peculiar discomfort, a kind of spiritual unease which I would banish as soon as possible.

One summer I was traveling in a foreign country, and, owing to an alteration in the railway time-table, I found myself obliged to change trains at a small lake-side town. As I had three hours to wait, I left the station and went out into the streets. It was an August afternoon, very hot and sultry, ominous thunder clouds were boiling up over the high mountains. At first I thought I would go down to the lake in search of coolness, but something ill-omened in the aspect of that stagnant sheet of lava-colored water repelled me, and I decided instead to visit the castle which was the principal feature of the place.

This ancient fortress was built at the highest point of the town and was clearly visible from the square in front of the station. It seemed to me that I had only to walk up any one of the steep streets leading in that direction to reach it in a few moments. But my eyes must have deceived me as to the distance, for it turned out to be quite a long walk. Arriving hot, tired and unaccountably depressed at the great studded gates, I almost decided not to enter, but a group of tourists was just going inside and I allowed the guide to pursuade me to join them.

I had been told at the station that the building now served as a museum, so it surprised me to see armed soldiers standing on guard in the courtyard. Replying to my question, the guide told me that part of the castle was still in use as a prison for offenders of a certain type. I tried to find out more as I had not heard before of these special prisons; the guide listened to me politely but refrained from answering. The other tourists, too, seemed to disapprove of my inquisitiveness. I gave in and became silent. We all trooped into a great hall and gazed at the dark stone walls carved in threatening relief.

As we went from one gloomy chamber to the next I wished more and more that I had not come on this expedition. The stone flags tired my feet, the menacing walls, the heavily barred doors, depressed my spirits; but I had the idea that it was impossible to go back, that no one would be permitted to leave these precincts until our guide led us outside again.

9

We were examining a display of medieval weapons when I noticed a small door half-hidden behind a suit of armor. I cannot tell now whether it was bravado, or a sudden longing for fresh air, or just idle curiosity that made me step behind the knight's ponderous armor and try the handle. To my astonishment the door was unlocked. It opened quite easily and I passed through it. The others, engrossed in the guide's lecture, paid no attention.

I was now in an enclosed flagged space, to small to be called a court, open to the sky, but so barricaded by cliff-like walls that no sunlight reached it and the livid air felt stale and oppressive. Not liking this any better than the interior of the castle, I was about to return to the tedious tour I had just forsaken, when something made me look down at the ground. I was standing in front of what I took for a low grating, a ventilator probably, which did not reach higher than the calf of my leg. Looking more attentively, I saw that this was in reality a low, barred window giving on to some subterranean cell. It was a movement behind the bars that had caught my eye. I knelt down, peering through the weeds which had grown up in the cracks between the great flag-stones.

At first I could see nothing, it might have been a black cellar into which I was gazing. But soon my eyes penetrated the darkness and I could make out some sort of a pallet under the grating with a shrouded form lying upon it. I could not be sure whether it was a man or a woman who lay there, shrouded as if on a bier, but I thought I discerned a tarnished gleam of fair hair, and presently an arm, no thicker than bone, was raised, feebly, as if groping towards the light. Was it imagination, or did I really see on that almost transparent flesh a faint stain, circular, toothed, and enclosing a shape like a rose?

I cannot hope that the horror of that moment will ever leave me. I opened my mouth, but for several seconds I was not able to utter a sound. Just as I felt myself about to call out to the prisoner, soldiers appeared and hustled me away. They spoke roughly and threateningly, jostling me and twisting my arms as they dragged me into the presence of their superior officer. I was commanded to produce my

11

passport. Falteringly, in the foreign language, I started to frame an inquiry about what I had seen. But then I looked at the revolvers, the rubber truncheons, the callous, stupid faces of the young soldiers, the inaccessible officer in his belted tunic; I thought of the massive walls, the bars, and my courage failed me. After all, what could I hope to do, an insignificant foreigner, and a woman at that, against such terrifying and strongly established force? And how would I help the prisoner by myself becoming imprisoned?

At last, after much questioning, I was allowed to go. Two guards escorted me to the station and stood on the platform until the train carried me away. What else could I have done? It was so dark in the underground cell: I can only pray that my eyes were deceiving me.

Going Up in the World

GOING UP IN THE WORLD

IN the low-lying streets near the river where I live there is fog all through the winter. When I go to bed at night it is so cold that the pillow freezes my cheek. For a long time I have been lonely, cold and miserable. It is months since I have seen the sun. Suddenly, one morning, all this becomes intolerable to me. It seems that I can no longer bear the cold, the loneliness, the eternal fog — no, not even for another hour — and I decide to visit my Patrons and ask them to help me. It is a desperate resolve, but once I have made it I am filled with optimism. Perhaps I deliberately trick myself with false hopes as I put on my best dress and carefully make up my face.

At the last moment, just as I am ready to start, I remember that I ought to take a present with me. I have no money with which to buy a gift worthy of such great people: is there anything in the house that will do? In a panic I hurry from room to room, as if expecting to discover some valuable object, the existence of which I have overlooked all the time I've been living here. Of course there is nothing suitable. Some apples on the kitchen shelf catch my eye because even in this gloomy half-light their cheeks show up yellow and red. I hastily fetch a cloth and polish four of the yellowest apples until they shine. Then I line a small basket with fresh paper, arrange the apples inside, and set out. On my way I tell myself that the simple fruit may please palates which have grown too accustomed to the flavor of hot-house peaches and grapes.

Soon I am in a lift, being whirled up towards the skies. A man-servant in white stockings and purple knee-breeches shows me into a magnificent room. Here one is above the fog, the sun is shining outside the windows draped in soft veils of net, or, if it is not, it makes no difference, for the room is full of artificial sunshine from the concealed lights. The floor is covered by a carpet softer than moss, there are chairs and great sofas upholstered in delicate brocade, beautiful flowers are arranged in vases some of which are shaped like shells and some like antique urns.

My Patrons are not present and I am in no hurry to meet them. I am happy just to be in this warm room with its sunny, flower-scented air through which one almost expects to see butterflies flitting. After the foggy gloom to which I have grown accustomed it is like being transported to summer, to paradise.

Before very long my Patron appears. He is tall and fine looking as such an important man ought to be. Everything about his appearance is perfect: his shoes gleam like chestnuts, his shirt is of finest silk, he wears a red carnation in his buttonhole and in his breastpocket is a handkerchief bearing a monogram embroidered by holy women. He greets me with charming courtesy and we sit talking for a while on general topics. He addresses me as an equal. I begin to feel quite elated at such a promising start. Surely everything is going to turn out as I wish.

The door opens and my Patroness enters. We both rise to meet her. She is dressed in deep blue velvet, and on her hat perches a small bird as vivid and rare as a jewel. There are pearls round her neck and diamonds on her smooth hands. She speaks to me with rather stilted brightness, smiling with narrow lips that do not unclose easily. Diffidently I offer my humble present, which is graciously accepted and then laid aside. My spirits fall somewhat. We sit down again in our cushioned seats and for a few minutes continue to maintain polite conversation. There comes a pause. I realize that the preliminaries are over and that it is time for me to state the object of my visit.

'I am freezing with cold loneliness down there in the fog!' I exclaim in a voice that stammers with its own urgency; 'please be kind to me. Let me share a little of your sunshine and warmth. I won't be any trouble to you.'

My companions glance at one another. A look of the deepest significance passes between them. I do not understand what the look means, but it makes me uneasy. It seems that they have already considered my petition and come to an understanding about it between themselves.

My Patron leans back in his chair and places the tips of his long fingers together. His cuff-links glitter, his hair shines like silk.

'We must treat this question objectively,' he begins. His voice has a reasonable, impartial sound, and I start to feel hopeful again. But as he goes on talking I perceive that the air of consideration which has impressed me so favorably is really nothing but a part of his perfect ensemble, and no more to be relied upon than the flower in his buttonhole. In fact, he is not to be trusted.

'Don't think that I am accusing you,' he says, 'or setting myself up as your judge, but you must admit that your conduct towards us in the past has been far from satisfactory.'

He looks again at my Patroness who nods her head. The little bird in her hat seems to wink at me with its brilliant, blind eyes.

'Yes,' says she, 'you have caused us a great deal of sorrow and anxiety by your bad behavior. You have never consulted our wishes about anything but have obstinately gone your own way. It is only when you are in trouble that you come here asking us to look after you.'

'But you don't understand,' I cry, and I am ashamed to feel tears in my eyes. 'It's a matter of life and death this time. Please don't bring the past up against me now; I'm sorry if I've offended you; but you have everything and you can afford to be generous. It can't mean very much to you. But, oh, if only you knew how I long to live in the sunshine again!'

My heart falls into my boots while I am speaking. I am plunged into despair because I see that neither of my hearers is capable of comprehending my appeal. I doubt if they are even listening to me. They do not know what fog is like; it is only a word to them. They do not know what it means to be sad and alone in a cold room where the sun never shines.

'We don't intend to be hard on you,' my Patron remarks, crossing his knees. 'No one will ever be able to say that we have not treated you with patience and forbearance. We will do our best to forget and forgive. But you, on your side, must promise to turn over a new leaf, to make a clean break with the past and give up your rebellious ways.'

His voice goes on, but now I am the one who is not listening. I have heard enough to fill me with hopeless disappointment. It is useless for me to attempt any further approach to people who are utterly inaccessible, utterly out of sympathy with me. Almost at my last gasp, I come to throw myself on their mercy, and a lecture is all they can find for me in their empty hearts. I sigh and undo my coat, which no one has invited me to remove, and in which I am now uncomfortably warm. My eyes glance sadly about the handsome room, in the golden, flowery atmosphere of which butterflies might be floating. Through a glaze of tears I catch sight of my yellow apples pushed into a corner behind an enormous box of liqueur chocolates. I feel remorseful because I have brought them here only to be abandoned to indignity. Perhaps the valet or the chambermaid will take a bite out of one of them before they are thrown into the dustbin.

'You must set out with the fixed intention of

doing your duty towards us,' my Patron is saying. 'You must try your hardest to wipe out past bad impressions. Above all you must demonstrate your gratitude towards your Patroness, earn her forgiveness, and prove yourslf worthy of her generosity.'

'And where am I to find a little warmth in all this?' I cry out desperately. What an incongruous sound the words have between these serene walls and how the fastidious flowers seem to toss their heads in disdain.

I know now that I have thrown away my last chance. There is no object in waiting a moment longer, so I get up and fly from the room. And at once the lift is swooping away with me, carrying me down to the cold, foggy streets where I belong.

The Enemy

THE ENEMY

SOMEWHERE in the world I have an implacable enemy although I do not know his name. I do not know what he looks like, either. In fact, if he were to walk into the room at this moment, while I am writing, I shouldn't be any the wiser. For a long time I believed that some instinct would warn me if we ever came face to face: but now I no longer think this is so. Perhaps he is a stranger to me; but much more probably he is someone whom I know quite well — perhaps someone I see every day. For if he is not a person in my immediate environment, how does he come to possess such detailed information about my movements? It seems quite impossible for me to make any decision — even concerning such a trifling matter as visiting a friend for the evening — without my enemy knowing about it and taking steps to ensure my discomfiture. And, of course, as regards more important issues, he is just as well informed.

Windsor Public Library

The fact that I know absolutely nothing about him makes life intolerable, for I am obliged to look upon everybody with equal suspicion. There is literally not a soul whom I can trust.

As the days go past I find that I am becoming more and more preoccupied with this wretched problem; indeed, it has become an obsession with me. Whenever I speak to anyone I catch myself scrutinizing him with secret attention, searching for some sign that would betray the traitor who is determined to ruin me. I cannot concentrate on my work because I am always debating in my mind the question of my enemy's identity and the cause of his hate. What act of mine can possibly have given rise to such a relentless persecution? I go over and over my past life without finding any clue. But perhaps the situation has arisen through no fault of my own but merely on account of some fortuitous circumstances that I know nothing about. Perhaps I am the victim of some mysterious political, religious or financial machination — some vast and shadowy plot, whose ramifications are so obscure as to appear to the uninitiated to be quite outside reason, requiring, for instance, something as apparently senseless as the destruction of everybody with red hair or with a mole on his left leg.

Because of this persecution my private life is already practically in ruins. My friends and family are alienated, my creative work is at a standstill, my manner has become nervous, gloomy and irritable, I am unsure of myself, even my voice has grown hesitating and indistinct.

You would think that my enemy might take pity on me now; that, seeing the miserable plight to which he has reduced me, he would be content with his vengeance and leave me in peace. But no, I know perfectly well that he will never relent. He will never be satisfied until he has destroyed me utterly. It is the beginning of the end now; for during the last few weeks I have received almost certain indications that he is starting to lodge false accusations against me in official quarters. The time can't be far off when I shall be taken away. It will be at night, probably, that they will come for me. There will be no revolvers, no handcuffs; everything will be quiet and orderly with two or three men in uniform, or white jackets, and one of them will carry a hypodermic syringe. That is how it will be with me. I know that I'm doomed and I'm not going to struggle against my fate. I am only writing this down so that when you do not see me anymore you will know that my enemy has finally triumphed.

A Changed Situation

A CHANGED SITUATION

WHEN one has lived for seven years in the same house some strange things are apt to take place. Of course, I am not speaking now about people who have lived all their lives in one house which they have perhaps inherited from their fathers and grandfathers or even from more remote ancestors: I imagine that an entirely different system of laws must apply to them. But when somebody like myself, a person who is by nature a wanderer, through a chain of accidental circumstances becomes attached to a certain building, the consequences may be very surprising.

I belong to a family of rolling stones. We have never been landowners; in fact, we have always avoided the accumulation of possessions which tend to restrict one's free movement about the world. So the prospect of becoming a householder gave rise to a good deal of talk among us.

My relatives all advised me to sell the property.

How I wish now that I had followed their advice! But at the time I was unaccountably averse to parting with the place. I remember that my uncle Lucius, who hates slow traveling, actually undertook a long, complicated cross-country journey — and in bitter Christmas weather, too — to come and discuss the matter with me. And I remember that I countered his reasonable proposals with arguments in which I only partially believed even then, saying that the house was too small to become burdensome and that if I sold it and invested the proceeds the income would be only negligible.

What made me so obstinate? That's the question I've asked myself hundreds of times without finding any answer. Was it a sort of masochism, a secret desire for self-punishment, that held me to a line of conduct which, right from the beginning, I more than half-consciously felt could only end in disaster?

It's not as though the place has any special attractions. It is a house of no definite architectural design, half old, half new. The lines of the new part are straightforward and easily read like a sum in simple arithmetic; the old part is complicated and oblique, full of treacherous angles, with a roof that sags like the back of a worn-out horse and is blotched with scabrous patches of lichen. Paradoxically, the old part has only been added recently. When I first came to live here it was an entirely new house — that is to say, it had certainly not been standing for more than ten or fifteen years. Now, at least half of it must have been built many centuries ago. It is the old part which has grown up during my occupation that I fear and distrust.

Lying peacefully curled up on a sunny day, the new house looks like a harmless gray animal that would eat out of your hand; at night the old house opens its stony, inward-turning eyes and watches me with a hostility that can scarcely be borne. The old walls drape themselves with transparent curtains of hate. Like a beast of prey the house lies in ambush for me, the victim it has already swallowed, the intruder within its ancient structure of stone.

Coiling itself round me it knows I cannot escape. Imprisoned in its very fabric, I am like a small worm, a parasite, which the host harbors not altogether unwillingly. The time has not yet come to eject me. A few more months or years the house will nourish me in its frozen bowels before it spews me like an owl's pellet into the arches of infinite space through which my husk of skin and crushed bones will fall for ever and ever.

Sometimes I almost burst out laughing when, in the level daylight, it turns its new face to me. Why this childish clinging to a pretense which misleads no one? Isn't it enough that the house has wound me with hateful entrails — that it will soon cast me out like vomit, like dung — but that it must even try to mock me with its deception as well?

Perhaps I do not catch a single glimpse of the ancient for days at a time. Only the tame gray animal confronts me, and seems as if it has rolled itself into a ball and is about to purr like a cat. Everything appears simple and above-board; but I am not taken in so easily. I watch, I am on the alert, I turn around suddenly to catch what is behind me. And sooner or later, sure enough, there, beyond the new innocuousness, is the old head rearing up like a hoary serpent, charged with antique, sly, unmentionable malevolence; waiting its time.

The Birds

THE BIRDS

IF some fortuneteller had predicted all the reverses I was to suffer this winter I should have laughed outright at such an exaggerated catalogue of evil. And yet, in point of fact, it would be almost impossible to exaggerate the number of misfortunes which have overtaken me during the last few months. And all due to the subterranean activities of a secret enemy whose very name is unknown to me! Could anything be more heart-breaking — more cruelly unfair? I am ready to burst into tears at the mere thought of such senseless injustice. But, of course, it's no good lamenting or making complaints or protestations to which nobody pays any attention and which may even, for all I know, be used against one in the ultimate issue.

It's this obscurantist atmosphere that is one of the worst aspects of the whole business. If only one knew of what and by whom one were accused, when, where, and by what laws one were to be judged, it would be possible to prepare one's defense systematically and to set about things in a sensible fashion. But as it is one hears nothing but conflicting rumors, everything is hidden and uncertain, liable to change at a moment's notice or without any notice at all.

How is it possible not to lose hope in these circumstances? As the days drag on without bringing forth anything more definite than a number of contradictory whispers or perhaps some equivocal and incomprehensible official communication of which one can't make head or tail, it's extremely difficult not to despair. One is forced into a position of inactivity, of passive waiting, of nerve-racking suspense, with absolutely no relief except an occasional visit to one's official advisor — an interview which is just as likely to plunge one into utter dejection as to buoy one up with fugitive hopes.

And through all this one is expected to carry on one's personal existence as usual; to work and to perform social and family duties as if the background of one's life were still perfectly normal: that is what is hardest of all to bear. Naturally one gets nervy and irritable and absent-minded; one's friends gradually start to avoid one; one's work suffers, and then one's health begins to break down. One loses sleep, it becomes harder and harder to take any interest in conversation, books, music, plays, eating and drinking, love-making, even in one's personal appearance. Ultimately one becomes completely cut off from reality, alone in a world in which there is nothing to do but wait, day after day, for some fate at which one can only guess but which, in any case, can scarcely be less tolerable than the preceding uncertainty.

That is the state of unreality in which I have been living now for some time. Perhaps it is not really so very long; perhaps not more than a month or so; one loses the sense of time as well as everything else in this wretched condition. It seems ages since I have been able to concentrate on my work: and yet I am obliged to put in the same number of hours each day at my desk.

What do I do with myself during these interminable hours which once used to pass so swiftly? My workroom overlooks a garden, a small green space containing three trees; a walnut, a cherry, and a third rather spindly tree, a variety of prunus, I fancy, of which I do not know the correct name though someone once told me that it was a Siberian plum. When life turns against one, one tends to seek a sort of timid solace in simple things, and I am not ashamed to admit that my principal occupation recently and almost my only pleasure has been connected with the birds which during the winter frequent this small enclosed piece of ground. I have taken lately to throwing out an occasional handful of grain onto the grass as well as scraps of bread and other food left over from the meals for which I no longer have any appetite. The weather all through January has been exceedingly cold — I can't help feeling that there is some connection between this bitter cold and my own sufferings — there has been snow on the ground practically continuously; a thing which I never remember seeing in previous winters. On account of these severe weather conditions an unusual number of small birds has congregated in the garden — great tits, blue tits, marsh tits, long-tailed tits, greenfinches and chaffinches, as well, of course, as robins, starlings, blackbirds, thrushes and innumerable sparrows.

A human being can only endure depression up to a certain point; when this point of saturation is reached it becomes necessary for him to discover some element of pleasure, no matter how humble or on how low a level, in his environment if he is to go on living at all. In my case these insignificant birds with their subdued colorings have provided just sufficient distraction to keep me from total despair. Each day I find myself spending longer and longer at the window watching their flights, their quarrels, their mouse-quick flutterings, their miniature feuds and alliances. Curiously enough, it is only when I am standing in front of the window that I feel any sense of security. While I am watching the birds I believe that I am comparatively immune from the assaults of life. The very indifference to humanity of these wild creatures affords me a certain safeguard. Where all else is dangerous, hostile and liable to inflict pain, they alone can do no injury because, probably, they are not even aware of my existence. The birds are at once my refuge and my relaxation.

A few days ago I was standing as usual in front of the window with my hands on the broad sill. It was the middle of the morning and I ought to have been at work, but a particularly hopeless mood of dejection had overtaken me and I had abandoned even the pretense of concentration. Perhaps you will wonder why I don't remember which day of the week it was: I can only answer that all days are so alike to me now that I really can't tell one from another. I remember that it was rather foggy, that the branches of the trees were motionlesss except when they were transiently stirred by the light weight of a bird, and that the half-frozen snow which had been lying about for so long, though not actually dirty, had acquired a sort of unsparkling deadness, very wearisome to the eye.

The woman who looks after me entered the room with some trivial message or question to which I replied without looking round. She is a good soul who has served me well for a number of years, but during the last few weeks a morbid sensitiveness has made it increasingly difficult for me to look her in the face. Does she know or does she not know the doom which is hanging over me? Sometimes I think she knows nothing; yet, surely, unobservant as she is, she must notice a change in me. And sometimes it seems to me that she goes out of her way to provide little tidbits for my meals, that she prepares my food with special care as if trying to tempt me to eat, and I fancy that I catch on her elderly face an expression that might almost be one of pity.

On this occasion of which I am writing I avoided her eye and continued to stare into the garden, feeling too miserable even to maintain before her a semblance of industry. And suddenly, my aimless gaze, shifting about the muffled, uncolored scene, was caught sharply and held amazed, incredulous, charmed, by an appearance so brilliant, so unexpected, that it was as if two tiny meteors of living flame had suddenly plunged through the dull atmosphere. It is impossible for me to describe adequately the vividness of those two small birds as they alighted among the sparse twigs of the prunus in the sad, misty half-light of the winter day. Not only their gay feathers, but their movements, their airy wing-sweeps, light as the pirouettes of extremely delicate dancers, gave an impression of unearthly buoyancy, of joyous animation that seemed to belong to visitants from a blither world.

I watched in astonishment, half believing myself the victim of a hallucination, expecting that next moment the birds would vanish away and leave the garden, unilluminated as before. But still they remained, not approaching the food which I had thrown out the window nor mingling with the other birds — now, by contrast, so drab and uninspired looking — but keeping to the straggly bare boughs of the prunus, sometimes flirting their wings as in an impish fan dance, sometimes comporting themselves with a mimic dignity, like cadets from the school of pages.

Enchanted by the vision, I was about to make an appreciative comment aloud, when something made me glance at the servant who was still standing behind me. Although she too was looking out into the garden, the good woman's face expressed no particular interest, and it was clear to me that she did not see the two bright birds which were causing me such emotion.

What conclusion was I to draw from this? It seemed incredible that anyone could fail to observe those twin spots of color, more striking than jewels on the gray January background. No, I could only presume that the birds were visible to me alone. That is the conclusion to which I have held ever since: for my ethereal visitors have not deserted me. It is true that several times in the day they will disappear, but always to return after a few hours, so that looking up from my papers I will suddenly be re-enheartened by the sight of their incongruous brightness in the midst of the dreary scene. Is this a good sign? I can almost bring myself to believe that it is; that an omen has been vouchsafed to me indicating that troubles are nearly over and that things are at last going to take a more favorable turn.

Or am I just being superstitious, like an unlucky gambler who sees fate in the fall of a chip and symbols even in the pattern of the wallpaper?

Airing a Grievance

AIRING A GRIEVANCE

YESTERDAY I went to see my official advisor. I have visited him fairly often during the last three months in spite of the inconvenience and expense of these interviews. When one's affairs are in such a desperate state as mine, one is simply obliged to make use of any possible help; and this man D has been my last hope. He has been the only source of advice and assistance available to me, the only person with whom I could discuss my affairs: in fact, the only person to whom I could speak openly about the intolerable situation in which I have been placed. With everybody else I have had to be reserved and suspicious, remembering the motto, 'Silence is a friend that never betrays anyone.' For how can I tell whether the person to whom I am talking is not an enemy, or perhaps connected with my accusers or with those who will ultimately decide my fate?

Even with D I have always been on my guard.

From the start there have been days when something seemed to warn me that he was not altogether to be trusted; yet on other occasions he filled me with confidence; and what was to become of me if I were deprived even of his support — unsatisfactory as it might be? No, I really couldn't face the future entirely alone, and so, for my own sake, I *must* not distrust him.

I went to him confidently enough in the first place. His name was known to me as that of a man, still young, but already very near the top of his profession. I considered myself lucky to have been placed in his charge, notwithstanding the long journey which separated me from him: in those early days I did not anticipate having to visit him frequently. At the beginning, I was favorably impressed by his solid town house, and by the room in which he received me with its wine-colored velvet curtains, its comfortable armchairs, its valuable looking pieces of tapestry.

About the man himself I was not so certain. I have always believed that people of similar physical characteristics fall into corresponding mental groups,and he belonged to a type which I have constantly found unsympathetic. All the same, there could be no doubt as to his ability, he was excellently qualified to take charge of my case, and as I was only to meet him occasionally — and then in a professional and not in a social capacity — the fact of our being basically antipathetic to one another seemed of little significance. The main thing was that he should devote sufficient time to my affairs, that he should study my interests seriously; and this, to begin with, he seemed quite prepared to do.

It was only later, as things went from bad to worse, and I was obliged to consult him at shorter and shorter intervals, that I started to feel dubious about his goodwill towards me.

At our early meetings he always treated me with extreme consideration, even with deference, listening with the closest attention to everything I had to say, and in general impressing me with the grave importance of my case. Irrational as it may sound, it was this very attitude of his — originally so gratifying — which aroused my first vague suspicions. If he were really looking after my interests as thoroughly as he asserted. why was it necessary for him to behave in this almost propitiatory way which suggested either that he was trying to distract my attention from some possible negligence on his part, or that matters were not progressing as favorably as he affirmed? Yet, as I have previously mentioned, he had a knack of inspiring confidence, and with a few encouraging, convincing phrases he could dispel all me tenuous doubts and fears.

But presently another cause for suspicion pricked my uneasy mind. Ever since my introduction to D I had been aware of something dimly familiar about his face with the very black brows accentuating deep-set eyes into which I never looked long enough or directly enough to determine their color but which I assumed to be dark brown. From time to time my thoughts idly pursued the half-remembered image which I could never quite manage to bring into full consciousness. Without ever really giving much attention to the subject, I think I finally decided that D must remind me of some portrait seen long before in a gallery, most probably somewhere abroad; for his countenance was decidedly foreign, and contained the curious balance of latent sensuality and dominant intellectualism seen to the best advantage in some of the work of El Greco. Then one day, just as I was leaving his house, the complete memory which had eluded me for so long, suddenly came to me with an impact sharp as a collision with a fellow pedestrian. It was no ancient portrait that D's face recalled to my mind, but a press photograph, and one that I had seen comparatively recently, one that was contained in an illustrated periodical which was probably still lying about somewhere in my living room.

As soon a I got home I started to search through the papers which, in my preoccupied state of mind, I had allowed to accumulate in an untidy pile. It was not long before I found what I was looking for. The face of the young assassin, gazing darkly at me from the page, was, in all essentials, the same black-browed face that had confronted me a short time previously in the curtained seclusion of his handsome room.

Why did this accidental likeness make such an impression on me, I wonder? Is it possible for a man to resemble a certain murderer in his outward appearance without possessing himself any violent tendencies; or if, as is more likely, he does possess them, without lacking sufficient restraint to hold them in check. One has only to think of D's responsible position, to look at the controlled, serene, intelligent face, to realize the fantastic nature of the comparison. The whole sequence of ideas is utterly grotesque, utterly illogical. And yet there it is; I can't banish it from my mind.

One must remember, too, that the man in the photograph was no common assassin, but a fanatic, a man of extraordinarily strong convictions, who killed not for personal gain, but for a principle, for what he considered to be the right. Is this an argument against D or in his favor? Sometimes I think one way, sometimes the other: I am quite unable to decide.

As a result of these prejudices — and of course there were others which would take too long to write down here — I decided to put my case in the hands of a different advisor. This was a serious step, not to be taken lightly, and I expended a great deal of time considering the subject before I finally sent off my application. Even after I had posted the letter I could not feel at all sure that I had done the right thing. Certainly, I had heard of people who changed their advisors, not once but several times, and of some who seemed to spend their whole time running from one to another: but I had always rather despised them for their instability, and the general feeling in the public mind was that the cases of these individuals would terminate badly. Still, on the whole, I felt that the exceptional circumstances warranted the change where I was concerned. In wording my letter of application I was particularly careful to avoid any statement that could possibly be taken as detrimental to D, merely stressing the point of how expensive and awkward it was for me to be continually undertaking the long journey to his house, and asking for my case to be transferred to someone in the university town near my home.

For several days I waited anxiously for an answer, only to receive at the end of that time a bundle of complicated forms to be filled up in duplicate. These I completed, sent off, and then waited again. How much of my life lately has consisted of this helpless, soul-destroying suspense! The waiting goes on and on, day after day, week after week, and yet one never gets used to it. Well, at last the reply came back on the usual stiff, pale blue paper, the very sight of which I have learned to dread. My request was refused. No explanation was given as to why a favor which had been granted to hundreds of people should be denied to me. But of course one can't expect explanations from these officials; their conduct is always completely autocratic and incalculable. All they condescended to add to the categorial negative was the statement that I was at liberty to dispense altogether with the services of an advisor should I prefer to do so.

I was so cast down after the receipt of this arbitrary communication that for two whole weeks I remained at home, absolutely inactive. I had not even the heart to go out of doors, but stayed in my room, saying that I was ill and seeing no one except the servant who brought my meals. Indeed the plea of illness was no untruth, for I felt utterly wretched in body as well as in mind, exhausted, listless and depressed as if after a severe fever.

Alone in my room, I pondered endlessly over the situation. Why, in heaven's name, had the authorities refused my application when I knew for a fact that other people were allowed to change their advisors at will? Did the refusal mean that there was some special aspect of my case which differentiated it from the others? If this were so, it must surely indicate that a more serious view was taken of mine than of the rest, as I was to be denied ordinary privileges. If only I knew — if only I could find out something definite! With extreme care I drafted another letter and sent it off to the official address, politely, I'm afraid even servilely, beseeching an answer to my questions. What a fool I was to humiliate myself so uselessly, most likely for the benefit of a roomful of junior clerks who doubtless had a good laugh over my laboriously-thought-out composition before tossing it into the wastepaper basket! Naturally, no reply was forthcoming.

I waited a few days longer in a state of alternate agitation and despair that became hourly more unbearable. At last — yesterday — I reached a point where I could no longer endure so much tension. There was only one person in the whole world to whom I could unburden my mind, only one person who might conceivably be able to relieve my suspense, and that was D who was still, when all was said, my official advisor.

On the spur of the moment I decided to go and see him again. I was in a condition in which to take action of some sort had become an urgent necessity. I put on my things and went out to catch the train.

The sun was shining, and I was astonished to see that during the period I had remained indoors, too preoccupied with my troubles even to look out of the window, the season seemed to have passed from winter to spring. When last I had looked objectively at the hills I had seen a Breughel-like landscape of snow and sepia trees, but now the snow had vanished except for a narrow whiteness bordering the northern edge of the highest point of the wood.

From the windows of the train I saw hares playing among the fine, emerald green lines of the winter wheat: the newly-ploughed earth in the valleys looked rich as velvet. I opened the carriage window and felt the soft rush of air which, not far away, carried the plover in their strange, reeling love dance. When the train slowed down between high banks I saw the glossy yellow cups of celandines in the grass.

Even in the city there is a feeling of gladness, of renewed life. People walked briskly towards appointments or dawdled before the shop windows with contented faces. Some whistled or sang quietly to themselves under the cover of the traffic's noise, some swung their arms, some thrust their hands deep in their pockets, others had already discarded their overcoats. Flowers were being sold at the street corners. Although the sunlight could not reach to the bottom of the deep streets the house-tops were brightly gilded, and many eyes were raised automatically to the burnished roofs and the soft, promising sky.

I, too, was influenced by the beneficient atmosphere of the day. As I walked along, I determined to put the whole matter of the letter and its answer frankly before D, to conceal nothing from him, but to ask him what he thought lay behind this new official move. After all, I had not done anything that should offend him; my request for a change of advisor was perfectly justifiable on practical grounds. Nor had I any real reason for distrusting him. On the contrary, it was now more than ever essential that I should have implicit faith in him, since he alone was empowered to advance my cause. Surely, if only for the sake of his own high reputation, he would do everything possible to help me.

I reached his house and stood waiting for the door to be opened. A beggar was standing close to the area railings holding a tray of matches in front of him, a thin, youngish man of middle-class appearance, carefully shaved, and wearing a very old, neat, dark blue suit. Of course, the whole town is full of destitute people, one sees them every-where, but I couldn't help wishing that I had not caught sight, just at this moment, of this particular man who looked as though he might be a schoolmaster fallen on evil days. We were so close together that I expected him to beg from me; but instead of that he stood without even glancing in my direction, without even troubling to display his matches to the passers-by, an expression of complete apathy on his face that in an instant began to dissipate for me all the optimistic influence of the day.

As I went inside the door, some part of my attention remained fixed on the respectable looking beggar, with whom I seemed in some way to connect myself. The thought crossed my mind that perhaps one day I, no longer able to work, my small fortune absorbed in advisor's fees, my friends irreparably alienated, might be placed in the same situation as he.

The manservant informed me that D had been called out on urgent business but that he would be back before long. I was shown into a room and asked to wait. Alone here, all my depression, briefly banished by the sun, began to return. After the spring-like air outside, the room felt close and oppressive, but a sort of gloomy inertia prevented me from opening one of the thickly draped windows. An enormous grandfather clock in the corner didactically ticked the minutes away. Listening to that insistent ticking, a sense of abysmal futility gradually overwhelmed me. The fact of D's absence, that he should choose today of all days to keep me waiting in this dismal room, created the worst possible impression on my over-wrought nerves. A feeling of despair, as if every effort I might make would inevitably be in vain, took possession of me. I sat lethargically on a straight-backed, uncomfortable chair with a leather seat, gazing indifferently at the clock, the hands of which had now completed a half circle since my arrival. I thought of going away, but lacked even the energy to move. An apathy, similar to that displayed by the beggar outside, had come over me. I felt convinced that already, before I had even spoken to D, the visit had been a failure.

Suddenly, the servant returned to say that D was at my disposal. But now I no longer wanted to see him, it was only with the greatest difficulty that

I forced myself to stand up and follow the man into the room where my advisor sat at his desk. I don't know why the sight of him sitting in his accustomed pose should have suggested to me the idea that he had not really been called out at all, but had been sitting there the whole time, keeping me waiting for some ulterior motive of his own; perhaps to produce in me just such a sensation of despair as I now experienced.

We shook hands, I sat down and began to speak, driving my sluggish tongue to frame words that seemed useless even before they were uttered. Was it my fancy that D listened less attentively than on previous occasions, fidgeting with his fountain pen or with the papers in front of him? It was not long before something in his attitude convinced me that he was thoroughly acquainted with the whole story of my letter of application and its sequel. No doubt the authorities had referred the matter to him — with what bias, with what implication? And now my indifferent mood changed to one of suspicion and alarm as I tried to guess what this intercommunication portended.

I heard myself advancing the old argument of inconvenience, explaining in hesitant tones that in order to spend less than an hour with him I must be nearly six hours on the double journey. And then I heard him answer that I should no longer have cause to complain of this tedious traveling, as he was just about to start on a holiday of indefinite length and would undertake no further work until his return.

If I felt despairing before you can imagine how this information affected me. Somehow I took leave of him, somehow found my way through the streets, somehow reached the train which carried me across the now sunless landscape.

How hard it is to sit at home with nothing to do but wait. I wait — the most difficult thing in the whole world. To wait — with no living soul in whom to confide one's doubts, one's fears, one's relentless hopes. To wait — not knowing whether D's words are to be construed into an official edict depriving me of all assistance, or whether he intends to take up my case again in the distant future, or whether the case is already concluded.

To wait — only to wait — without even the final merciful deprivation of hope.

Sometimes I think that some secret court must have tried and condemned me, unheard, to this heavy sentence.

Just Another Failure

JUST ANOTHER FAILURE

I WAS feeling very anxious and unhappy when I left D's house, angry with myself and with him as well because he had refused to help me. It was quite natural that I should have gone to him in my distress. He certainly knows more than any living person about me and my affairs, he is a clever man whose judgment is to be trusted, and also, on account of his profession, he has special qualifications for advising on problems of this sort.

'Why won't you tell me what I ought to do?' I asked him indignantly at the end of our interview. 'Why can't you give me a definite line of conduct and save me from all this suffering and uncertainty?'

'That's exactly what I don't intend to do,' he answered me. 'The trouble with you is that you're always avoiding responsibility. This is a case where you must act on your own initiative. I'm sorry if I appear unkind, but you must believe me when I say that it will do you far more good in the long run to see this through by yourself than blindly to follow outside advice — whether mine or anyone else's . . .'

I was so hurt by D's unexpected attitude that I believe I was thinking more about him than about my own trouble as I went out into the wintry London twilight. In my imagination I kept hearing his agreeable, soft, sympathetic voice, so out of keeping with the heartless words it was speaking, and seeing his dark-browed face which always vaguely reminded me of some other face I had seen long ago, I couldn't remember quite where, perhaps in a painting or a newspaper photograph. I felt mortified at having asked him for a favor which he was unwilling to give. I was ashamed of having presumed too much on a friendship which might, all the time, have been a very one-sided affair. Quite possibly I had allowed my own wishes to delude me into mistaking that sympathetic manner of his for the sign of some warmth of feeling towards me personally. Now that I came to consider it, I could not recall a single occasion during our acquaintanceship when his behavior had expressed anything more than the generalized benevolence of a humane, understanding and intelligent man. The idea of having made such a mistake was specially distressing to me because I am by nature very reserved and afraid of receiving rebuffs from the people around me. Now I felt that I had given myself away and that D must be despising me or laughing at me; though really I knew perfectly well that he understood the workings of the mind and heart too clearly to be guilty of that sort of cruelty.

Although these humiliating thoughts were far from pleasant, I clung to them as long as possible, actually exaggerating to myself my own recent mortification, as if my relations with D were of more importance than anything else in the world. But of course I couldn't succeed in driving the real problem out of my head. It was there all the time, like a toothache which gradually grows more and more insistent until it finally drowns every other sensation.

What was I going to do about the interview at which I was shortly supposed to be present? The questions I had so desperately put to D and which he had refused to answer, now presented themselves to me with imperious urgency. Should I go to the hotel, as I had agreed to do, to meet my husband and the young woman whom he proposed to introduce into our home? Was I capable of accepting emotionally the situation to which, in discussion, I had already given an intellectual acceptance? With what smile, with what words, should I greet this stranger, younger, more beautiful, more fortunate than I? With what unnaturally hardened gaze should I observe glances, gestures, long familiar to my heart, directed towards a new recipient?

The recurring sequence of these questions, to which I seemed fundamentally incapable of replying — to which, indeed, I did not hope or expect to find any answers — began to assume by its very monotony a quality of horror and torment impossible to describe. I began to feel that if I did not succeed in breaking out of the loathsome circle I should suddenly become mad, scream, perpetrate some shocking act of violence in the open street. But worst of all was the knowledge that the laws of my temperament would forbid me even a relief of this kind; that I was inexorably imprisoned behind my own determination to display no emotion whatever.

I was cold and tired. I realized that I must have been walking for a long time without taking any notice of my direction. Now I saw that I was in a street which I did not know very well. Night had fallen, the lights glowed mistily through a thin haze. I looked at my watch and saw that the hour arranged for the interview had almost arrived.

No sooner had I discovered this than a change seemed to come over everything. It was as though, in some mysterious way, I had become the central point around which the night scene revolved. People walking on the pavement looked at me as they passed; some with pity, some with detached interest, some with more morbid curiosity. Some appeared to make small, concealed signs, but whether these were intended for warning or encouragement I could not be sure. The windows lighted or unlighted, were like eyes more or less piercing, but all focused upon me. The houses, the traffic, everything in sight, seemed to be watching to see what I would do.

I turned round and began to walk quickly in the direction of the hotel. I hurried in order not to be late for my appointment, but the idea of taking a taxi for some reason never ocurred to me. The attention of the city accompanied me as I went, the bright eyes of the cars followed me faithfully, with speculation or foreknowledge. In my head I could hear D's pleasant voice telling me that I must act on my own initiative. His face, with the black eyebrows that always recalled an elusive memory, floated before me, no larger than a mouse, and then vanished away.

I came to the hotel entrance which was brilliantly lighted. People were going in and out of the revolving doors. I walked slower and finally stood still. Even now I half believed that I should go inside, keep the appointment, and behave creditably, too, at the interview. But then my feet were carrying me away, and I knew, what I think the watching eyes had known all the time, that rather than face the situation I would escape anywhere, into no matter what shame, what guilt, what despair.

Shall I be able to endure my self-condemnation now? But that is only a rhetorical question, because, although it is difficult to live with so much unhappiness and so many failures, to die seems to be harder still.

The Summons

THE SUMMONS

R IS one of my oldest friends. Once, long ago, we used to live in flats in the same building, and then, of course, I saw a great deal of him. Afterwards the circumstances of our lives altered, wider and wider distances divided us, we could only meet rarely and with difficulty — perhaps only once or twice in a whole year — and then only for a few hours or at most for a weekend. In spite of this our friendship — which was purely platonic — continued unbroken, although it was naturally not possible to maintain quite the original degree of intimacy. I still felt that a close and indestructible understanding existed between R and myself: an understanding which had its roots in some fundamental character similarity and was therefore exempt from the accidents of change.

A particularly long interval had elapsed since our last encounter, so I was delighted when we were at length able to arrange a new meeting. It was settled that we should meet in town, have dinner together, and travel by train later in the evening to the suburb where R was living.

Our appointment was for seven o'clock. I was the first to arrive at the restaurant, and, as soon as I had put my bag in the cloakroom, I went upstairs to the little bar which I often visited and where I felt quite at home. I noticed that a waiter was helping the usual barman, and in the idle way in which one's thoughts run when one is waiting for somebody, I wondered why an assistant had been brought in that evening, for there were not many customers in the bar.

R appeared almost immediately. We greeted each other with happiness, and at once fell into a conversation which might have been broken off only the previous day.

We sat down and ordered our drinks. It was the waiter and not the barman who attended to us. As the man put down the two glasses on the table, I was struck by his ugliness. I know that one should not allow oneself to be too much influenced by appearances, but there was something in this fellow's aspect by which I couldn't help feeling repelled. The word 'troglodyte' came into my head as I looked at him. I don't know what the cave dwellers really looked like, but I feel that they ought to have been very much like this small, thick-set, colorless individual. Without being actually deformed in any way, he seemed curiously misshapen; perhaps it was just that he was badly-proportioned and rather stooping. He was not an old man, but his face conveyed a queer impression of antiquity; of something hoary and almost obscene, like a survivor of the primitive world. I remember particularly his wide, gray, unshaped lips which looked incapable of anything so civilized as a smile.

Extraordinary as it seems, I must have been paying more attention to the waiter than to my friend, for it was not until after we had lifted our glasses that I noticed a certain slight alteration in R's appearance. He had put on a little weight since our previous meeting and looked altogether more prosperous. He was wearing a new suit too, and when I complimented him upon it, he told me that he had bought it that day out of a considerable sum of money which he had received as an advance on his latest book.

I was very glad to hear that things were going so well with him. Yet at the same time a small arrow of jealousy pierced my heart. My own affairs were in such a very bad way that it was impossible for me not to contrast my failure with his success, which seemed in some indefinable manner to render him less accessible to me, although his attitude was as friendly and charming as it had ever been.

When we had finished our drinks we went down to the restaurant for dinner. Here I was surprised, and, I must admit, rather unreasonably annoyed, to see the same waiter approaching us with the menu. 'What, are you working down here as well as upstairs?' I asked him, irritably enough. R must have been astonished by my disagreeable tone, for he looked sharply at me. The man answered quite politely that his work in the bar was finished for the evening and that he was now transferred to the restaurant. I would have suggested moving to a table served by a different waiter, but I felt too ashamed to do so. I was very mortified at having made such an irrational and unamiable display of feeling in front of R, who, I felt sure, must be criticizing me adversely.

It was a bad start to the meal. All on account of this confounded waiter, the evening had acquired an unfortunate tendency, like a run of bad luck at cards which one cannot break. Although we talked without any constraint, some essential spark, which on other occasions had always been struck from our mutual contact, now withheld from us its warmth. It even seemed to me that the food was not as good as usual.

I was glad when the waiter brushed away the crumbs with his napkin and set the coffee before us. Now at last we should be relieved of the burden of his inauspicious proximity. But in a few minutes he came back, and putting his repulsive face close to mine, informed me that I was wanted outside in the hall.

'But that's impossible — it must be a mistake. Nobody knows I'm here,' I protested: while he

unemphatically and obstinately insisted that someone was asking for me.

R suggested that I had better go and investigate.
So out I went to the hall where several people were
sitting or standing about, waiting to meet their
friends. I could see at a glance that they were all
strangers to me. The waiter led me up to a man of
late middle age, neatly and inconspicuously
dressed, with a nondescript, roundish face and a
small gray moustache. He might have been a bank
manager or some such respectable citizen. I think he
was bald headed. He bowed, and greeted me by
my name.

'How do you know who I am?' I asked in amaze-
ment. I was positive that I had never seem him
before: yet how could I be quite certain? His was one
of those undistinguished faces which one might see
many times without remembering it.

In reply, he began to reel off quite a long speech;
but all so fast and in such a low voice that I could
only catch a word here and there and these did not
make sense. Totally unable to follow what he was
saying, I only vaguely got the impression that he

was asking me to accompany him somewhere. Suddenly I saw that the suitcase standing on the floor near his feet was my own.

'What are you doing with my bag? How did you get it . . .? The attendant had no right to let you take it out of the cloakroom,' I said angrily, stretching down for the handle. But before I could reach it he picked up the bag himself with a deprecating smile, and carried it out of the door.

I followed him, full of indignation and eager to reclaim my property. In the street, pedestrians came between us and I was unable to catch up with him until he had turned the corner into a narrow alley full of parked cars. It occurred to me that the man was out of his mind: I couldn't believe he intended to steal the suitcase; he looked far too respectable for that.

'What's the meaning of all this? Where are you taking my bag?' I said, catching hold of his sleeve. We were just beside a large black limousine which stood in the rank of waiting cars. My companion rested the bag on the running board.

'I see that you haven't understood me,' he said:

and now for the first time he spoke clearly so that I could really hear what he was saying. 'Here is my authorization. It was merely out of consideration for you that I refrained from producing it inside where everyone would have seen it.' He took a pale blue form out of his pocket and held it towards me. But in the uncertain cross-light from the street lamps and the cars I only had time to make out some unintelligible legal phrases, and my own name embellished with elaborate scrolls and flourishes in the old-fashioned style, before he hastily put the stiff paper away again.

I was opening my mouth to ask him to let me look at it properly, when the chauffeur of the black car suddenly climbed out of the driving seat and picked up my case with the clear intention of putting it inside the vehicle.

'That belongs to me — kindly leave it alone!' I commanded, at the same time wondering what I should do if the man refused to obey my order. But, as if the whole matter were of perfect indifference to him, he at once let go the handle and returned to his seat where he immediately appeared to become absorbed in an evening newspaper.

Now for the first time I observed the official coat-of-arms emblazoned on the glossy black door panel of the car, and I saw too that the windows were made of frosted glass. And for the first time I was aware of a faint anxiety; not because I thought for an instant that the situation was serious, but because I had always heard what a tedious, interminable business it was to extricate oneself from official red tape once one had become even remotely involved with it.

Feeling that there was not a moment to be lost, that I must make my explanations and escape before I became any further entangled in this ridiculous mesh of misunderstanding, I began to talk to the elderly man who was standing patiently beside me. I spoke quietly and in a reasonable tone, telling him that I was not blaming him in the least, but that a mistake had certainly been made; I was not the person mentioned on the document he had shown me which probably referred to somebody of the same name. After all, my name was not an uncommon one; I could think of at least two people offhand — a film actress and a writer of short stories — who were called by it. When I had finished speaking I looked at him anxiously to see how he had taken my arguments. He appeared to be impressed, nodded his head once or twice in a reflective way, but made no reply. Encouraged by his attitude, I decided on a bold move, picked up my suitcase and walked rapidly back to the restaurant. He did not attempt to stop me, nor as far as I could see, was he followng me, and I congratulated myself on having escaped so easily. It seemed as if boldness were what was most needed in dealing with officialdom.

R was still sitting at the table where I had left him. My spirits had now risen high. I felt cheerful, lively and full of confidence as I sat down — bringing my bag with me this time — and related the peculiar incidents that had just taken place. I told the story quite well, smiling at the absurdity of it; I really think I made it sound very amusing. But when, at the end, I looked for R's smile of appreciation, I was astonished to see that he remained grave. He did not look at me, but sat with downcast eyes, drawing an invisible pattern on the cloth with his coffee spoon.

'Well — don't you think it was funny that they should make such a mistake?' I asked, trying to force his amusement.

Now indeed he looked up at me, but with such a serious face and with eyes so troubled, that all my assurance and good spirits suddenly evaporated into thin air. Just at that moment I noticed the ugly waiter hovering near, almost as if he were trying to overhear our conversation, and now a feeling of dread slowly distilled itself in my veins.

'Why don't you say something?' I burst out in agitation as R still remained silent. 'Surely it's not possible that you think — that there was no mistake ...? That I am the person they really wanted?'

My friend put down the spoon and laid his hand on my arm. The affectionate touch, so full of sympathy and compassion, demoralized me even more than his words.

'I think, if I were you,' he said slowly and as if

with difficulty, 'I think I would go and find out just what the charge is against you. After all, you will easily be able to prove your identity if there has really been a mistake. It will only create a bad impression if you refuse to go.'

Now that I have so much time on my hands in which to think over past events, I sometimes wonder whether R was right: whether I would not have done better to keep my freedom as long as possible and even at the risk of prejudicing the final outcome of the affair. But at the time I allowed him to persuade me. I have always had a high opinion of his judgment, and I accepted it then. I felt, too, that I should forfeit his respect if I evaded the issue. But when we went out into the hall and I saw the neat, inconspicuous man still impassively, impersonally waiting, I began to wonder, as I have wondered ever since, whether the good opinion of anybody in the whole world is worth all that I have had to suffer and must still go on suffering — for how long; oh, for how long?

At Night

AT NIGHT

HOW slowly the minutes pass in the winter night: and yet the hours themselves do not seem so long. Already the church clock is calling the hour again in its dull country voice that sounds half stupified with the cold. I lie in bed, and like a well-drilled prisoner, an old-timer, I resign myself to the familiar pattern of sleeplessness. It is a routine I know only too well.

My jailer is in the room with me, but he cannot accuse me of being rebellious or troublesome. I lie as still as if the bed were my coffin, not wishing to attract his attention. Perhaps if I don't move for a whole hour he will let me sleep.

Naturally, I cannot put on the light. The room is as dark as a box lined with black velvet that someone has dropped into a frozen well. Everything is quiet except when the house bones creak in the frost or a lump of snow slides from the roof with a sound like a stealthy sigh. I open my eyes in the darkness. The eyelids feel stiff as if tears had congealed upon them in rime. If only I could see my jailer it would not be so bad. It would be a relief to know just where he is keeping watch. At first I fancy that he is standing like a dark curtain beside the door. The ceiling is lifted off the room as if it were the lid of a box and he is towering up, taller than an elm tree, up towards the icy mountains of the moon. But then it seems to me that I have made a mistake and that he is crouching on the floor quite close to me.

An iron band has been clamped round my head, and just at this moment the jailer strikes the cold metal a ringing blow which sends needles of pain into my eye sockets. He is showing his disapproval of my inquiring thoughts; or perhaps he merely wishes to assert his authority over me. At any rate, I hastily shut my eyes again, and lie motionless, hardly daring to breathe, under the bedclothes.

To occupy my mind I begin to run through the formulas which the foreign doctor taught me when I first came under suspicion. I repeat to myself that there is no such person as a *victim* of sleeplessness,

94

that I stay awake simply because I prefer to continue my thoughts. I try to imagine myself in the skin of a newborn infant, without future or past. If the jailer looks into my mind now, I think, he cannot raise any objection to what is going on there. The face of the Dutch doctor, thin and sharp and hard like the face of a sea captain, passes before me. Suddenly a cock crows nearby with a sound fantastic, unearthly, in this world still locked in darkness and frost. The cock's crow flowers sharply in three flaming points, a fiery fleur-de-lis blossoming momentaneously in the black field of night.

Now I am almost on the point of falling asleep. My body feels limp, my thoughts start to run together. My thoughts have become strands of weed, of no special color, slowly undulating in colorless water.

My left hand twitches and again I am wide awake. It is the striking of the church clock that has called me back to my jailer's presence. Did I count five strokes or four? I am too tired to be certain. In any case, the night will be over soon. The iron band on my head has tightened and slipped down so that it presses against my eyeballs. And yet the pain does not seem so much to come from this cruel pressure as to emanate from somewhere inside my skull, from the brain cortex: it is the brain itself which is aching.

All at once I feel desperate, outraged. Why am I alone doomed to spend nights of torment, with an unseen jailer, when all the rest of the world sleeps peacefully? By what laws have I been tried and condemned, without my knowledge, and to such a heavy sentence, too, when I do not even know of what or by whom I have been indicted? A wild impulse comes to me to protest, to demand a hearing, to refuse to submit any longer to such injustice.

But to whom can one appeal when one does not even know where to find the judge? How can one ever hope to prove one's innocence when there is no means of knowing of what one has been accused? No, there's no justice for people like us in the world: all that we can do is to suffer as bravely as possible and put our oppressors to shame.

An Unpleasant Reminder

AN UNPLEASANT REMINDER

LAST summer, or perhaps it was only the other day
— I find it so difficult to keep count of time now —
I had a very disagreeable experience.

The day was ill-omened from the beginning; one
of those unlucky days when every little detail seems
to go wrong and one finds oneself engaged in a
perpetual and infuriating strife with inanimate
objects. How truly fiendish the sub-human world
can be on these occasions! How every atom, every
cell, every molecule, seems to be leagued in a
maddening conspiracy against the unfortunate
being who has incurred its obscure displeasure! This
time, to make matters worse, the weather itself had
decided to join in the fray. The sky was covered with
a dull gray lid of cloud, the mountains had turned
sour prussian blue, swarms of mosquitoes infested
the shores of the lake. It was one of those sunless summer days that are infinitely more de-
pressing than the bleakest winter weather; days

when the whole atmosphere seems stale, and the world feels like a dustbin full of cold battered tins and fish scales and decayed cabbage stalks.

Of course, I was behindhand with everything all day long. I had to race through my changing for the game of tennis I had arranged to play in the afternoon, and as it was I was about ten minutes late. The other players had arrived and were having some practice shots as they waited for me. I was annoyed to see that they had chosen the middle court which is the one I like least of the three available for our use. When I asked why they had not taken the upper one, which is far the best, they replied that it had already been reserved for some official people. Then I suggested going to the lower court; but they grumbled and said that it was damp on account of the over-hanging trees. As there was no sun, I could not advance the principal objection to the middle court, which is that it lies the wrong way for the afternoon light. There was nothing for it but to begin playing.

The next irritating occurrence was that instead of keeping to my usual partner, David Post, it was for some reason decided that I should play with a man named Müller whom I hardly knew and who turned out to be a very inferior player. He was a bad loser as well, for as soon as it became clear that our opponents were too strong for us, he lost all interest in the game and behaved in a thoroughly unsporting manner. He was continually nodding and smiling to the people who stopped to watch us, paying far more attention to the onlookers than to the game. At other times, while the rest of us were collecting the balls or I was receiving the service, he would move away and stare at the main road which runs near, watching the cars as if he expected the arrival of someone he knew. In the end it became almost impossible to keep him on the court at all; he was always wandering off and having to be recalled by our indignant shouts. It seemed futile to continue the game in these circumstances, and at the end of the first set we abandoned play by mutual consent.

You can imagine that I was not in a particularly good mood when I got back to my room. Besides being in a state of nervous irritation I was hot and tired, and my chief object was to have a bath and change into fresh clothes as soon as possible. So I was not at all pleased to find a complete stranger waiting for me to whom I should have to attend before I did anything else.

She was a young woman of about my own age, quite attractive in a rather hard way, and neatly dressed in a tan linen suit, white shoes, and a hat with a little feather. She spoke well, but with a slight accent that I couldn't quite place: afterwards I came to the conclusion that she was a colonial of some sort.

As politely as I could I invited her to sit down and asked what I could do for her. She refused the chair, and, instead of giving a straightforward answer, spoke evasively, touching the racket which I still held in my hand, and making some inquiry about the strings. It seemed quite preposterous to me in the state I was in then to find myself involved with an unknown woman in an aimless discussion of the merits of different makes of rackets, and I'm afraid I closed the subject rather abruptly and asked her point-blank to state her business.

But then she looked at me in such a peculiar way, saying in quite a different voice, 'You know, I'm really sorry I have to give you this,' and I saw that she was holding out a box towards me, just an ordinary small, round, black pillbox that might have come from any druggist. And all at once I felt frightened and wished we could return to the conversation about tennis rackets. But there was no going back.

I'm not sure now whether she told me in so many words or whether I simply deduced that the judgment which I had awaited so long had at last been passed upon me and that this was the end. I remember — of all things! — feeling a little aggrieved because the sentence was conveyed to me in such a casual, unostentatious way, almost as if it were a commonplace event. I opened the box and saw the four white pellets inside.

'Now?' I asked. And I found that I was looking at my visitor with altered eyes, seeing her as an official messenger whose words had acquired a fatal portentousness.

She nodded without speaking. There was a

pause. 'The sooner the better,' she said. I could feel the perspiration, still damp on me from the game, turning cold as ice.

'But at least I must have a bath first!' I cried out in a frantic way, clutching the clammy neck of my tennis shirt. 'I can't stay like this — it's indecent — undignified!'

She told me that would be allowed as a special concession.

Into the bathroom I went like a doomed person, and turned on the taps. I don't remember anything about the bath; I suppose I must have washed and dried myself mechanically and put on my mauve silk dressing gown with the blue sash. Perhaps I even combed my hair and powdered my face. All I remember is the little black box confronting me all the time from the shelf over the basin where I had put it down.

At last I brought myself to the point of opening it and holding the four pills on the palm of my hand; I lifted them to my mouth. And then the most ridiculous contretemps occurred — there was no drinking glass in the bathroom. It must have got broken: or else the maid must have taken it away and forgotten to bring it back. What was I to do? I couldn't swallow even four such small pellets without a drink, and I couldn't endure any further delay. In despair I filled the soapdish with water and swallowed them down somehow. I hadn't even waited to wash out the slimy layer of soap at the bottom and the taste nearly made me sick. For several times I stood retching and choking and clinging to the edge of the basin. Then I sat down on the stool. I waited with my heart beating as violently as a hammer in my throat. I waited; and nothing happened; absolutely nothing whatever. I didn't even feel drowsy or faint.

But it was not till I got back to the other room and found my visitor gone that I realized that the whole episode had been a cruel hoax, just a reminder of what is in store for me.

Machines in the Head

MACHINES IN THE HEAD

THERE is some quite trivial, distant noise; a sound, moreover, which has nothing to do with me, to which there is not the slightest need for me to pay any attention: yet it suffices to wake me, and in no gentle way, either, but savagely, violently, shockingly, like an air raid alarm. The clock is just striking seven. I have been asleep perhaps one hour, perhaps two. Roused in this brutal fashion, I jump up just in time to catch a glimpse of the vanishing hem of sleep as, like a dark scarf maliciously snatched away, it glides over the foot of the bed and disappears in a flash under the closed door. Useless, quite futile, to dash after it in pursuit: I am awake now for good, or rather, for bad; the wheels, my masters, are already vibrating with incipient motion; the whole mechanism is preparing to begin the monotonous, hateful functioning of which I am the dispirited slave.

'Stop! Wait a little — it's so early — Give me a little respite!' I cry, although I know it is quite in vain: 'Only let me have a little more sleep — an hour — half an hour — that's all I ask.'

What's the good of appealing to senseless machinery? The cogs are moving, the engines are slowly gathering momentum, a low humming noise is perceptible even now. How well I recognize every sound, every tremor of the laborious start. The loathsome familiarity of the routine is almost the worst part of it, intolerable and inescapable at the same time, like a sickness inside the blood. This morning it drives me to rebellion, to madness; I want to batter my head on the walls, to shatter my head with bullets, to beat the machines into pulp, into powder, along with my skull.

'It's horribly unjust!' I hear myself calling out — to what, to whom, heaven alone knows. 'One can't work so many hours on so little sleep. Doesn't anyone know or care that I'm dying here amongst all these levers and wheels? Can't somebody save me? I haven't really done anything wrong — I feel terribly ill — I can hardly open my eyes —'

And it's true that my head aches abominably and I feel on the point of collapse.

Suddenly I notice that the light which hurts my eyes so much comes from the sun. Yes, the sun is actually shining outside, instead of snow there is dew sparkling all over the grass, crocuses have spread their neat, low fire of symmetrical flames under the rose bushes. Winter has gone; it is spring. In astonishment I hurry to the window and look out. What has happened, then? I feel dazed, bewildered. Is it possible that I am still living in a world where the sun shines and flowers appear in the springtime? I thought I had been exiled from all that long ago. I rub my tired eyes; still there is sunlight, the rooks flap noisily about their nests in the old elms, and now I hear how sweetly the small birds are singing. But even as I stand there all these happy things start to recede, to become phantasmal, transparent as the texture of dream plasma, banished by the monstrous mechanical outlines of pulleys, wheels, shafts, which in their orderly, remorseless and too-well-known evolutions now with increasing insistence demand my attention.

Like a fading mirage in the background I can

still, straining my eyes, faintly discern the sunlit grass, the blue, blue arches of sky across which a green shape flies in remote parabola, the ghost of an emerald dagger spectrally flung.

'Oh, stop — stop! Give me another minute — just a minute longer to see the green woodpecker!' I implore with my hands already, in automatic obedience, starting to perform their detested task.

What does a machine care about green woodpeckers? The wheels revolve faster, the pistons slide smoothly in their cylinders, the noise of machinery fills the whole world. Long since cowed into slavish submission, I still draw from some inexorable source the strength to continue my hard labor although I am scarcely able to stand on my feet.

In a polished surface of metal I happen to notice my reflected face; it wears a pale, beaten lonely look, eyes looking out at nothing with an expression of fear, frightened and lonely in a nightmare world. Something, I don't know what, makes me think of my childhood; I remember myself as a schoolchild sitting at a hard wooden desk, and then as a little girl with thick, fair, wind-tossed hair, feeding the swans in a park. And it seems both strange and sad to me that all those childish years were spent in preparation for this — that, forgotten by everybody, with a beaten face, I should serve machinery in a place far away from the sun.

Asylum Piece

ASYLUM PIECE

I

THE scene is set exactly like a stage upon which a light comedy, something airy and gay, is about to be acted. At the back can be seen part of the ground floor of a mansion with doors right and left opening upon a wide terrace where tables and chairs are arranged. In front, a flight of shallow stone steps leads down to the garden. Large pillars of light-colored stone support the roof of the terrace. At each end, beyond the final column, the walls of the house can be seen covered by creepers which are a mass of brilliant orange and purple flowers. Some of the full-blown flower trumpets have been carried by the wind on to the steps where they lie as if strewn for the feet of a bridal procession. The foreground, which in a theater would be the auditorium, consists of an enormous view over falling ground with a lake in the middle distance and mountains beyond. The whole vista is flooded with dazzling midsummer sunshine.

At first there is no one to be seen. A flock of pigeons circles round twice with flashing wings and vanishes into the upper blue.

The door at the right extremity of the terrace opens and a number of people emerge. They are well-dressed men and women of varying ages who stand about or sit in groups round the tables. They have just finished lunch. Some are smoking, some have coffee cups in their hands. The most striking thing about them is their silence. Only a few talk together; the others seem abstracted, or as if suspended, as if waiting to be told what to do. After a few moments they start to drift slowly across the terrace and vanish one after another through the door on the left. A gray-haired woman who appears to be in a position of authority is seen to be shepherding them along. She settles a group of four at a table on the extreme left and gives them a pack of cards which one of them deals in a perfunctory fashion.

A stout man in a dark suit occupies the most

comfortable chair in the middle of the terrace. He is about forty years old, slightly bald, and has a round, red, cheerful face. He unfolds a newspaper and starts to read. Something, it is not easy to say what, distinguishes him from the people who have lately passed by. Perhaps it is merely that he is exempt from the domination of the gray-haired woman. He is the Professor.

After a minute or two, the door on the left opens and three new figures emerge with a somewhat stealthy appearance: they have an obvious air of having evaded authority. At the sight of the Professor, whom they had not expected to find there, they hesitate uncertainly, but he smiles at them over his paper and waves them forward with an indulgent gesture. Relieved, they advance past the card players, who glance up at them with faint curiosity, and then seat themselves on the top step of the terrace just in front of the Professor.

Here they remain for a while without speaking, staring through their dark glasses into the glare. The central person of the trio is a young woman with yellow hair. She is smartly dressed in pale pink. On her right is a young man with the pointed ears and the half wistful, half malicious look of a faun. The man on her other side is older with a sad Jewish face. Between all three a curious resemblance is noticeable, and this is not only due to the fact that each one is slender and elegant and wearing a pair of dark spectacles.

The card players, having once displayed their dim inquiry, without further interest in what is passing lethargically continue the game which they have been ordered to play, dealing and receiving the cards with gestures as automatic as those of the hands of so many clocks. The Professor rustles the page of his newspaper. The three on the steps sit motionless, deriving some incommunicable solace from each other's proximity and from the fugitive sense of escape.

Suddenly a flock of pigeons flies up from the direction of the lake and circles low in front of the terrace with bright flashing wings. And immediately, as if stricken into life at the sight of those beating wings, the three rise from the steps with one simultaneous lamentable cry.

Now it can be seen only too clearly where their mutual and horrid resemblance lies. What appeared as slender elegance now reveals itself as emaciation, hip bones protrude shockingly through the covering clothes, cheekbones have almost pushed their way through the reluctant flesh.

The long, lank, match-thin limbs with their enlarged joint mechanisms jerk into forlorn obedience to the Professor's wires as, like a smiling puppet-master, he hurriedly takes control. And from behind the three pairs of dark spectacles large tears roll over the painted marionette cheeks and slowly drip onto the stone terrace.

ASYLUM PIECE

II

I HAD a friend, a lover. Or did I dream it? So many dreams are crowding upon me now that I can scarcely tell true from false: dreams like light imprisoned in bright mineral caves; hot, heavy dreams; ice-age dreams; dreams like machines in the head. I lie between the bare wall and the medicine bitter with sediment in its dwarfish glass, and try to recall my dream.

I see myself walking hand-in-hand with another, a human being whose heart and mind had grown into mine. We walked together on many roads, in sunshine beside ancient olive trees, on hillsides sprayed as by fountains with the larks' singing, in lanes where the raindrops dripped from the chilly leaves. Between us there was understanding without reservations and indestructible peace. I, who had been lonely and incomplete, was now fulfilled.

Our thoughts ran together like greyhounds of equal swiftness. Perfection like music was in our united thoughts.

I remember an inn in some southern country. A crisis, long since forgotten, had arisen in our lives. I remember only the cypresses' black flames blowing, the sky hard as a blue plate, and my own confidence, serene, unshakable, utterly secure. 'Whatever happens is trivial so long as we are together. Under no circumstances could we fail one another, wound one another, do one another wrong.'

Who shall describe the slow and lamentable cooling of the heart? On what day does one first observe the infinitesimal crack which finally becomes a chasm deeper than hell?

The years passed like the steps of a staircase leading lower and lower. I did not walk anymore in the sun or hear the songs of larks like crystal fountains playing against the sky. No hand enfolded mine in the warm clasp of love. My thoughts were again solitary, disintegrate, disharmonious — the music gone. I lived alone in a few pleasant rooms, feeling my life run out aimlessly with the tedious hours: the life of an old maid ran out of my fingertips. I arranged the flowers in their vases.

Yet still, intermittently, I saw him, the companion whose heart and brain once seemed to have grown to mine. I saw him without seeing him, the same and yet not the same. Still I could not believe that everything was lost beyond hope of salvage. Still I believed that one day the world would change color, a curtain would be ripped away, and all would be as it once was.

But now I am lying in a lonely bed. I am weak and confused. My muscles do not obey me, my thoughts run erratically, as small animals do when they are cornered. I am forgotten and lost.

It was he who brought me to this place. He took my hand. I almost heard the tearing of the curtain. For the first time in many months we rested together in peace.

Then they told me that he had gone. For a long while I did not believe it. But time passes by, and no word comes. I cannot deceive myself any longer. He has gone, he has left me, and he will not return.

I am alone forever in this room where the light burns all night long and the professional faces of strangers, without warmth or pity, glance at me through the half-open door. I wait, I wait, between the wall and the bitter medicine in the glass. What am I waiting for? A screen of wrought iron covers the window; the house door is locked though the door of my room is open. All night long the light watches me with its unbiased eye. There are strange sounds in the night. I wait, I wait, perhaps for the dreams that come so close to me now.

I had a friend, a lover. It was a dream.

ASYLUM PIECE

III

HANS comes out of the lift and crosses the hall of the clinic. Just beside a large vase of salmon-pink gladioli which stands on a table, he remembers that he has left the door of the lift open. He turns back and closes it very carefully, then slowly crosses the wide hall again. He is a small, slim man, quite young, with pointed ears and black hair that grows in a point on his forehead. His brown eyes, which nature intended to be gentle and mischievous, are now gentle and sad. His whole expression is one of barely concealed anxiety which shows also in the undecided steps of his shiny black shoes. He is smartly, if rather unsuitably, dressed in a dark town suit.

A woman in a white uniform wishes him good morning from her desk near the main door. He answers mechanically, without seeing her. At the door he hesitates for several moments: it is difficult for him to pass through it although it is standing open. Finally he manages to overcome his inhibition and goes outside. On the steps he again hesitates, not being able to decide which direction to take.

The sun shines brilliantly. Before him is a park-like expanse of grass with groups of trees and some single fine Wellingtonias dotted about. There is nobody in sight. It is eleven o'clock and all the patients who are well enough are at work in the atelier or in different parts of the grounds.

Hans glances round uneasily. It is part of his routine, too, to work in the atelier at this hour. Until a few days ago someone would certainly have come to investigate his absence: but now nobody comes near him; nobody seems to care how he occupies his time. This strikes him as exceedingly ominous. 'My brother must have written to say that he can't afford to keep me here much longer. Soon I shall be sent away from the clinic — and then what will become of me?'

He sighs and takes from his pocket a crumpled

letter which he has been carrying about for several days. It is from his brother in Central Europe and contains nothing but bad news about the factory upon which the family fortune depends — strikes, unemployment, rising price of raw materials. The whole village also depends upon the factory; the whole village is suffering.

Hans sighs again deeply and returns the letter to his pocket without unfolding it. He takes out his dark spectacles and puts them on, hiding from the brightness of the day which fills him with obscure alarms.

Suddenly his face changes. A girl of about twenty is approaching him on a bicycle. She is the gymnastic teacher with whom, up to a few days ago, Hans has been indulging in a mild flirtation. Now he feels far too anxious to think of flirting, although he admires automatically the beautiful golden tan of her bare arms and legs. She carries a black swimming suit over the handlebars of her cycle.

'How I wish she would ask me to go swimming with her!' he thinks to himself, as a smile of eager anticipation appears on his face. It is not that he really wants to swim in the lake; but what he longs for above everything at this moment is laughter, companionship and a friendly voice.

The girl is abreast of him now; her thick, curly hair blows out like a fleece in the sun. The gravel crunches, minute particles of grit fly up from under the tires; there is a greeting, a flash of teeth and a whirring noise. She has gone.

Hans stands for a moment watching the departing form of the gym mistress. The smile slowly fades from his face and he begins to walk on. His loitering steps carry him as a matter of course in the direction of the atelier. On his way he passes the vegetable garden where several patients are working. Two of them, in blue overalls, are hoeing the parched earth quite close to the path where he walks. A man nearby, who looks like a gardener, is really a nurse who is keeping them under his eye. Hans pauses to watch the workers who do not return his gaze. The ground is baked dry, it is hard work, sweat runs down their faces. The two men do not speak to each other, nor do they look happy; yet Hans, who detests hard work, almost envies them their place in the established order of institutional life to which he now feels himself an outsider. He wanders on past another man who is picking blackberries. The blackberry bushes have been trained over wires, and the patient stands with his back to Hans, intent on his prickly task, carefully picking out the berries and putting them into a basket. Hans would like to speak to him, but the unresponsive look of the man's back deters him, and he walks on in silence, looking abstractedly at the path.

His thoughts fall back into their usual unhappy pattern — money troubles, bad health, insecurity. Once more he fingers the letter in his pocket. Yes, the poor old factory is certainly in a bad way — perhaps even on its last legs. How brokenhearted father would have been! A good thing the old man didn't live to see these terrible times. But what about Han's own enterprise, the small private business which he has built up by his personal efforts? For the hundredth time he tries to think of some reason why he has not heard from his partner for such a long time. It's over a month since the fellow has written. 'Can he be ill? Is he double-crossing me? Or has he really written and they have kept the letters from me because of more bad news? I really ought to go and find out what's happening. I ought to go at once — tomorrow. If I wait I may be too late.' But the thought of taking a long train journey alone, of talking to strangers and concentrating upon business problems, is too much for poor Hans. 'I can't do it. It's no use. They shouldn't expect it of me in my condition. I'm ill — I can't sleep, I can't eat, I can't make decisions. I can't even think properly anymore . . .' He passes his hand over his dark hair with a despairing gesture, takes off his glasses for a moment, and then, dazzled, hastily puts them back on his nose.

Now he has reached the atelier. A confused hum of activity comes from within. In the carpenter's shop someone is hammering. A machine in one of the other rooms makes a thin buzzing noise like a wasp. The various workshops open onto a veranda raised several steps above the path where Hans is walking, but looking up he can see the faces of the people near the windows and doors.

131

With some of them he exchanges a nod. They are busy with book-binding or leather-work or basket-making. The official in charge of the atelier comes out onto the veranda for a minute to wish Hans good day. He behaves as though it were quite in order for him to be strolling out there when all the rest of the clinic is hard at work. This attitude on the part of the supervisor confirms the young man's worst fears as he moves off immediately.

At the last open door a girl is sitting alone, working at a sketch on an easel. 'Hullo, Hans!' she calls out amiably.

He stops and leans against the stone wall of the veranda. He would like to see what she is painting, but the effort required to mount the steps is too great, and he stays where he is, looking up at her wistfully.

'Why do you always wear those dark clothes? — she asks him. 'You look so hot and dismal — as if you were going to a funeral or a dreary business appointment.'

'Well, you see, it's like this,' he begins to explain, feeling the stone warm under the palms of his hands, 'I never could decide what to put on. Every morning when I started to dress I used to put out all my suits in a row, and it would take me perhaps half an hour, perhaps longer, to make up my mind. The same thing happened with my shoes — with my ties — it was really awful. You can't think how this silly affair used to worry me. So at last I thought of a plan to avoid making a choice. I just put on the same suit every day. This is the one I wore when they took us to that concert in Geneva; I've worn it ever since.'

The girl doesn't say any more. She doesn't see his forlorn expression. Perhaps she is not interested; perhaps her painting absorbs her just then; or perhaps she has simply fallen into a dream.

Hans moves away. Suddenly he feels envious, bitter. 'She's well — not nearly as ill as I am, at any rate. And yet she can stay here as long as she likes while I shall be turned out in a day or two to face the world.'

So far he has been dawdling along, but now he comes to a decision and starts to walk briskly. He will send another telegram to his partner and this time he will word it so that it is bound to bring a reply. Out he goes into the dusty public road that leads to the village. He has no business to be there, but what does it matter? He has often done it before, and anyway, nobody seems to care what he does these days.

Soon he comes to the street of humble, rather squalid houses, shuttered against the heat. Most of the dwellings are built in one with their cowsheds or stables. In front of one an enormous heap of manure slowly steams in the sun. The overpowering smell of manure, the heat, the quick walk, combine to make Hans feel dizzy for a few seconds. He stands still, bending his head, and looking down at his shoes, now white like a tramp's with the dust. With fumbling fingers he unfastens his jacket. A tiny split in the front of his shirt catches his eye. 'But I'm going about in rags — absolutely in rags! It will be the gutter for me next,' he mutters under his breath, with a sort of mild, aggrieved surprise.

Now he is at the post office. He pulls himself together and goes inside. The empty room smells fustily of dried ink, just outside the window some shabby, gaunt hens are pecking in an enclosure of wire netting overgrown with convolvulus. Hans observes with distaste all the details of the place with which he is already too familiar. The postmaster appears. He is an oldish, pot-bellied peasant with grizzled hair. Carefully, with much thought, Hans writes out his message and hands the telegraph form over the counter.

After the young man has gone, the postmaster stands for a time holding the telegram against his huge belly, and watching the door as if he half expects the sender to come back. Then, in a methodical way, he sets about tearing the form into small pieces, until nothing is left but a handful of shreds which he negligently tosses out of the open window. With greedy eyes, the hens come rushing on their strong, scaly legs, pouncing on the torn fragments. But immediately discovering that the paper scraps are inedible, they abandon them in disgust and resume their unprofitable pecking in the hard earth.

ASYLUM PIECE

IV

AN elderly man and his wife are standing in the chief doctor's study. The husband is a big, tall man who is beginning to stoop a little. He has a serious, important face with a large gray moustache and pouches under the eyes. In his buttonhole he wears a narrow red ribbon. He is rather a fine figure for his age and is obviously used to being in a position of command. His wife, on the other hand, is non-descript and ineffective looking. One realizes at once that she has been dominated by her husband ever since their marriage, and by her parents before that.

It is just after noon on a hot summer day. The interview is ended. The chief doctor rises behind his desk. He is as tall as his visitor, but handsome, slender and in the prime of life, with thick, wavy hair which he wears rather long and which is just starting to be becomingly streaked with gray. He is dressed in a beautiful silver-gray suit and brown and white shoes. The room is large, lofty and expensively furnished, but rather dark with curtains drawn over the french windows. There is a perceptible odor of eau de cologne ambrèe which emanates from the doctor's person. One feels that a slightly mysterious atmopshere has been aimed at with a view to impressing visitors. There are flowers and a number of large, dim, allegorical pictures.

The couple move slowly towards the door. The wife is distressed and reluctant to leave. There is something she wants to say, but she is intimidated by the atmosphere of the room and by the doctor who looks to her like a film actor. Finally she manages to bring out a question.

'Couldn't I please, doctor, see her just for a minute before we go? We've come all this way — and it's such a long time since I saw her . . .' Her voice, just as one would expect, is humble and diffident. The poor old lady is tired out with traveling and not far from tears as she stands there nervously clasping her shapeless black handbag and gazing at the head doctor with imploring eyes.

'My dear madame, it would be the greatest mistake. It would upset your daughter and possibly cause a relapse. I'm extremely sorry, but we must consider the patient's best interests before everything, mustn't we? I assure you that she has settled down most satisfactorily, I am very pleased with her progess, and I have excellent reports of her from my doctors as well. You can leave her in our hands without the slightest anxiety. She is well and happy and has taken remarkably well to our community life.'

The cultured voice sounds softer than silk, but the mother hardly hears the last part of the speech. She grasps only that she is not to be permitted to see her child who is so close to her, perhaps even within calling distance, hidden away behind all these invisible barriers of medical authority and discipline. A mist comes in front of her eyes, she can no longer see very clearly where she is going; but this does not matter because her husband takes her by the arm and steers her firmly through the door.

'We must be guided in everything by the doctor's advice,' he is saying. And then she hears him refusing an invitation to lunch at the chief's private house. 'A thousand thanks — no. We shall just be in time to catch the express from Lausanne.'

Tremulously, she walks down the polished corridor, supported by the inexorable arm of her husband. She does not see the white-coated attendant who is escorting them. She feels very old, and chilly in spite of the heat. Now there is nothing before her but the tiresome, exhausting train journey back to her empty home.

The head doctor is relieved to have got rid of the elderly pair. He had quite expected that he would have to entertain them to lunch. As soon as he ceases to hear the sound of the car carrying them away, he opens a window and steps out into the sunshine. His house is a short distance off, on the shore of the lake. As he walks towards it, everyone whom he passes stops to salute and admire the fine-looking, clever, successful, debonair physician with his graceful, athletic stride.

Meanwhile, Mademoiselle Zèlie is getting ready

for lunch in her own room. She is a plump, heavy-looking girl in the early twenties, who has rather the air of an enormously bloated child. Her body seems unwieldy like a young child's, and her face has the childish simplicity that includes some cunning. Her complexion is pale and unhealthy, her hair needs a shampoo. She has altogether a rather slatternly aspect: her stockings are wrinkled, there is a gap at the back between her white linen skirt and her spotted blouse. Her nurse, who is sitting over some embroidery at the window, suddenly takes a look at her, jumps up and impatiently rearranges her clothing.

'How is it you can't keep yourself tidy, mademoiselle?' she says in a scolding voice. 'I'm always putting you right and you're as bad again in two minutes. Your hair, too — you haven't combed it yet. And your hands — have you washed them for lunch? Let me look — no, of course not. Go on now, give them a good scrub with the brush; the nails are quite black.' And she gives the girl a little push towards the washbasin.

Zélie obediently turns on the taps. As the water

140

is running into the basin, she glances at her companion with dislike. This is a new nurse: her nurses never stay long with her. 'Why does she nag at me like that?' she is thinking. 'To have one of these stupid creatures with me all the time, day and night . . . their stupid voices going on and on . . . just peasant women, too, who don't understand anything — it's insupportable. If only my mother would come . . . If only I could tell her . . . She would never allow it.'

Standing there with her hands in the water she has quite forgotten what she is supposed to be doing. The nurse comes up with the expression of a person restraining herself in exasperating circumstances, lets out the water, gives her a towel and briskly and efficiently tidies her hair. 'There, now; we must hurry. The gong's gone — didn't you hear it?'

Zèlie is glad to go into the dining room; she is fond of her food. But today her pleasure is spoilt by the fact that her place has been laid next to a young Italian whom she detests. As she sits down between him and her nurse, she glances with sidelong suspicion at the shock-headed, narrow-eyed youth who teases her and confuses her with his spiteful tricks.

Today it seems as though he is going to leave her in peace. He says nothing at all until the first course has been eaten and taken away. Then, just as the waiters are making a subdued clatter with the fresh plates, he leans towards her and whispers into her ear: 'And how were your mother and father today, mademoiselle?'

'My mother and father? They haven't been here.' She looks at him blankly, yet with distrust, out of her sparkless eyes.

'Oh, yes, indeed — they were here this morning. I was in the corridor when they came out of the doctor's study. He was saying good-bye to them. I saw them and heard the name quite distinctly.' The Italian boy seems to be only interested in his food, but really he is all attention, all on the alert.

Zèlie takes a mouthful of veal from her plate. Suddenly she grasps the meaning of what has just been said to her; the implication of the words dawns upon her. She lets her knife and fork fall.

'My mother has been here . . . and she went away . . . without seeing me!'

Her chair is on the side of the table nearest the double doors. The doors are almost immediately behind her chair. She has only to get up and take two or three steps and then she is out of the room. For a moment everything hangs in suspense. The waiters stand poised with their dishes. There has been no noise, no disturbance: for a moment no one seems to realize what has happened. Then the girl's nurse rises and follows her. Here and there about the room other figures also get to their feet and go out. The young Italian bends low over his plate. His mouth is crammed full of food, his jaws solemnly chewing. But an impish glee crinkles the ends of his eyes: his is happy.

Zèlie runs across the hall towards the chief doctor's study. The main door of the clinic is wide open and her pursuers will naturally assume that she has gone out that way. It is not with the idea of eluding them that she goes to the study, but simply because the Italian said that he had seen her mother there. Of course, the room is now empty; but the

143

french window is still open as the doctor left it, and Zèlie passes through it. Now she is on a grass bank that slopes down to a pine wood. She runs down the steep bank, moving clumsily, tripping and stumbling in her high-heeled shoes which do not fit very well. In the wood she still finds it hard to run because the pine needles are slippery, and treacherous roots are continually tripping her up. She is out of condition and soon feels exhausted. Her breath makes a painful sobbing sound in the quiet wood, her heartbeats sound loud and continuous like a waterfall, her face, streaked with her tumbled hair, is glazed over with sweat, one of her shoes has gone and she is completely disheveled. She does not know why she is running or where. One word, 'Mother! Mother!' keeps crying out in her head.

Suddenly she is pulled up short. A wire fence, twelve feet high and strong enough to imprison a herd of wild beasts, marks the boundary of the estate. Zèlie is running so blindly that she does not see the wire and crashes against it. Her hands beat on the fine mesh, her awkward body staggers and falls to the ground. She lies collapsed on the pine needles under the indifferent trees. The small harmony of the wood, which her clumsy irruption has broken, slowly renews itself. A wood pigeon starts to coo over her head. That gentle summer sound, which when she was a child always made her think of her mother's sewing machine, is more than Zèlie can bear. Her heart breaks, she clutches handfuls of the sharp pine needles which pierce her flesh, while from between her thick lips, smeared with saliva and rouge, issues a desolate keening that soon leads her pursuers in the right direction.

ASYLUM PIECE

V

IT is quite early, just after seven o'clock, on a beautiful summer morning. The sky is pale blue, cloudless, serene and mild, like an immense arch, not awe-inspiring, but full of benevolence and protectiveness. The untroubled lake is opalescent, half-solid looking as if one could walk across it. The mountains withdraw their stern faces behind gauzy mist veils. On the first slope of the hillside above the lake the main building of the clinic stands washed in the clear new sunshine, a fine mansion with flowers edging the balconies and a pillared terrace in front. Everything is peaceful, orderly and reassuring. In a steep hayfield above the road some laborers are already at work with their scythes, moving rhythmically, their brown, nude torsos gleaming like statuary. A car comes along the highroad from the town and smoothly loops its way up the private road to the clinic. It stops in front of the main entrance which is in shadow, on the side of the building that faces away from the lake. Here the aspect of the new day is slightly less comfortable, owing perhaps to the dark, wide shade from the house and the huge black trees that point severely away from the world.

A man and a young woman emerge from the car. They have been traveling all night. The man is about forty, rather well looking in the heavy Roman emperor style, young for his age, in spite of the fact that his face is unshaven and wears a harassed expression. He has the indescribably, almost imperceptibly, false look of a person who is outwardly friendly and kind but inwardly barren and self-absorbed. He is large, and altogether somewhat disheveled after the journey. The woman, who is several years younger than he, is almost in a state of collapse and has to be helped up the steps into the clinic. Nevertheless, she has managed to achieve a fairly normal appearance. Her green dress is in order, her fair hair is smoothly combed, there is powder on her face and lipstick on her mouth:

probably her last living impulse would be to attend to these things. She does not speak or look about her, but passively allows herself to be led into a room facing the lake where there is sunshine and a large vase of antirrhinums on a round table. Here she subsides onto a sofa. The pupils of her eyes are dilated, she sees only a blur of afflicting brightness, she is really hardly conscious of what is going on. The man sits in a chair near her, drumming nervously on the table with this thick fingers. Neither of the two utters a word.

A girl in a white overall brings in a tray of coffee. She is attractively fresh looking and glances with curiosity at the travel-worn strangers, particularly at the woman who now seems to be on the verge of losing consciousness altogether and falling off the sofa onto the floor. The attendant speaks to her, pours out a cup of coffee and puts a cushion under her head. With colossal effort the other pulls herself back to life sufficiently to murmur some half-audible comment, shading her eyes with her hand. The nurse goes to the window and quietly closes the shutters: then she goes out of the door with a last backward glance. Now there is only a green, subaqueous dimness left in the room, striated with bands of brightness. The man, in unbroken silence, and, as it were, gloomily, apprehensively, absent-mindedly, swallows the hot coffee, directing from time to time upon his companion a look of automatic anxiety which really conceals a sort of resentment. The other cup of coffee, untasted, slowly steams on the table.

After a few minutes the chief doctor comes into the room. Although it is so early in the morning, he is immaculately turned out and has an air of brisk and vital efficiency about his handsome person. He shakes hands with the visitor who rises to greet him, immediately sinking back heavily into his chair. Then the doctor goes to the fair-haired woman and takes her limp hand. There is an exchange of preliminary talk between the two men. The stranger briefly outlines certain medical details with which the physician has already been made familiar by letter. The large man speaks in the halting manner of someone who forces himself to discuss a matter subconsciously repugnant to him. He often fails to finish a sentence, one gets the impression that his real attention is wandering, that he longs to dissociate himself from the whole situation. The doctor, although he listens with polite attention, realizes that the other, unable or unwilling to acknowledge responsibility, will say nothing of any value, and his dark eyes continually turn to the silent woman across the room. Finally he addresses her:

'So you think you would like to come to my clinic, madame?'

She, who has appeared oblivious of the talk, reacts unexpectedly to the direct question. Her eyes open wide, a kind of contortion appears on her face as though she might weep or even strike a blow if she had the strength. She pulls herself up on the sofa, clenches her hands, and her voice too is unexpectedly strong as she answers:

'No, I never wanted to come. I was forced — brought here against my will.'

She cannot help the intense hostility in her tone, which is the result of hysteria, of complete emotional exhaustion, perhaps of despair: it is aimed at her own neurosis and at a whole chain of events which have gone before — not at the man who now speaks to her with a smile. But he, because they are foreigners and strangers to one another, and because they belong besides to ethnological groups fundamentally unsympathetic, he is a little stung, a little displeased. However, he continues to smile as he says with unchanging smoothness:

'Perhaps you will rest here for a few minutes. There are one or two things I must discuss with monsieur.'

Left alone, the young woman lapses into a state of complete quiescence, her fair hair spread on the brown cushion. She does not move, she hardly appears to breathe; only at long intervals a deep, broken sigh comes from her painted lips, her gray, distracted, unfocused eyes open wide and gaze at the pleasant room like the eyes of a lost person, a person who has lost his memory, or has been incomprehensibly taken prisoner in a strange land.

The two men are absent rather a long time, at least half an hour, but she does not notice. It would be all the same to her if they stayed away the whole morning: drugs and exhaustion have destroyed her appreciation of time. She is not asleep, but neither is she truly awake. Vague fantasies, most of them unpleasant, occupy her submerged brain.

Presently the big man returns with a nurse. The doctor sends a message that he has been called away but will visit his new patient later in the morning. Supported by the two others, the young woman slowly traverses a wide corridor. Now there are signs of life in the building. A few patients, accompanied by an attendant, are returning from the gymnasium. Some of them look curiously at the blonde victim, soon to be their companion, who does not return their gaze: most likely she does not see them. The man with her is clearly uneasy, frowning and biting his nails, and seeking security in talk with the tranquil, matter-of-fact nurse in her white overall.

Now they are in a bedroom. The nurse goes in search of the luggage. The other woman, her last physical force depleted by the recent exertion, droops on the edge of the bed, less than half present: only a kind of mechanical masochism still keeps her upright. Her companion, without knowing why, is irritated by this posture.

'Why don't you lie down comfortably?' he asks her, repressing annoyance and keeping his voice low.

She does not answer, but something — perhaps it is the sight of the white clouds that now, like choir boys, like seraphs, are moving across the sky in ordered procession — moves her to take his hand.

'I'll get better now ... Everything will be all right, won't it?' she says, incoherent, seeking from him some reassurance which is not in his power to give.

He stirs awkwardly, scowling and biting the nails of his free hand.

'Yes ... of course ... you'll get better ...' He only wants to be free, to be gone — anywhere, out of this situation so intolerable to his irresponsible heart. But suddenly he bends down and kisses her on the cheek. She is surprised out of her trance, touched, grateful, encouraged; for a second she feels almost her old self. Even now, at the last moment, she will save everything; she will walk, and they

153

will go out together into the sun. She starts to speak, to stand up, but he disengages himself and goes to the door.

'You're going away?' she asks, disappointed. He mutters something, looking aside. 'But you'll come back soon?'

'Yes, of course. When you're in bed.'

He goes out of the room. She sits on the edge of the bed, suspended, almost lifeless, the brief animation, departed, leaving her emptier than before.

All at once she hears the engine of a car being started outside. From where she is sitting she can see through the window covered with iron scrolls, a sweep of the drive where a car is beginning to move. Her eyes recognize that it is the car in which they drove from the town, but her brain draws no conclusion from this. Suddenly she sees in the back seat the man who accompanied her. But even now she feels only bewilderment, stupefaction. What does it mean? Why is he in the car? His suitcase lies on the seat at his side, and for some reason the sight of this bag, which she herself gave him years before, convinces her of the truth.

'He's leaving me here. He's going away ...
Without telling me ... Without even a word.
When he kissed me it was good-bye.'

Some final desperate reserve of nervous energy
enables her to run to the door. 'I must go to him — I
must stop him — he can't leave me like this!' she
cries out to the empty room. The door is locked on
the outside. She twists the handle and beats on the
glass panel. The glass is unbreakable and an iron bar
would do no more than splinter it. Nevertheless she
continues to beat weakly upon it with her two hands
while tears run down her distorted face.

An attendant passing along the corridor glances
with a startled look at the convulsed face with its
wild, lost, streaming eyes, and then hurries off in
search of someone in authority.

ASYLUM PIECE

VI

IT is early in the morning in one of the bedrooms of the foreign clinic. The empty room has the indefinably forlorn air of a place just deserted by its usual occupant. The door into the passage stands open, there is a tray with disarranged breakfast things on a table beside the bed. The room is quite large and has a parquet floor and well-proportioned furniture of pale wood: although one would not call it luxurious, it is certainly comfortable and pleasant. All the same, there is something a little odd, a little disquieting, about it. It would be difficult to locate the source of this impression; perhaps the circumstance that there is not a single hook anywhere, that all planes are bare and smooth, and that the electric light is protected by a wire screen, has something to do with it. The big window, too, is covered by a grille of wrought iron work which, though it is ornamental, somehow suggests a utilitarian purpose. Just now the room is cool, even chilly, in spite of the fact that it is midsummer. There is a thick white mountain mist out of doors.

A young peasant girl in an overall hurries in from the passage, carries away the breakfast tray, and then returns with an armful of cleaning utensils. She is nineteen or twenty years old, big, robust, rather bony, with an unbeautiful large-nosed face and brown hair scraped back from her forehead. All her movements are clumsy but vigorous. She kneels down on the floor, scoops a dollop of some thick, greaselike substance out of a tin, and begins to polish the boards energetically. As she works she quietly hums to herself a long, tuneless national song. All her life she has worked hard, she is full of unbounded energy, it pleases her to see the smooth wood shine like water under her cloth; she is happy.

Soon the floor is polished as if for a ball, but still there is the bed to make, the furniture to attend to. She washes her hands at the basin and dries them on her special cloth before putting the bed in

157

order: then goes over to dust the dressing table, looking with unenvious curiosity at the decorative boxes of powder and cream, the scent in its slender flask.

Before she has finished, the occupant of the room returns from her bath. She is about ten years older than the peasant girl, of whom she is the antithesis in every way; the two might serve as examples of opposite products of society. The newcomer is exceedingly slim and decorative in a sophisticated way. Her long, smoothly curving, heavy blonde hair, her full cyclamen-colored gown that trails on the floor, give her a somewhat romantic appearance which is not negatived by her unhappy eyes, nor by her face of assumed hardness, of assumed indifference, which does not conceal desolation.

She says good morning, then carelessly drops on the bed the sponge, the soap, the essence which she has brought back from the bath, and goes to the window where she stands staring out at the mist that hides everything behind its sad, opaque, colorless veil. The peasant girl hurries to pick up the things from the bed and arranges them carefully in their proper places. As she finishes her work she glances all the time at the other woman who stands there so still, looking away from her, as if in another world. The graceful cyclamen robe fills the beholder with admiration. 'How wonderful it must be to wear such a dress,' she thinks in her simple heart. 'She looks like an angel with her hair hanging down so bright': and she touches her own drab head with a sort of surprise.

'The room is done now,' she says at length, timidly, in the bad French which she speaks only with difficulty.

The woman in front of the window makes no reply, no movement at all. Perhaps she has not understood, perhaps she has not heard.

The other takes out her brooms, her cloths, her polish, and puts everything down in the corridor. Then she goes back and loiters a moment or two inside the bedroom door. She knows she ought to get on with her work, to hurry into the next room and start polishing the floor there, instead of wasting her time; but somehow she cannot bear to go away without some response from that motionless figure whose hands are now clutching the scrolls of the iron grille.

'Don't stand there, madame,' she says in her awkward way; 'madame will catch cold — let me close the window.' She crosses the room and actually reaches towards the glass, brushing the other's sleeve as she does so. The physical touch breaks the spell of the elder woman's abstraction and she turns her head. The servant is horrified to see her eyes overflowing with tears which slowly and without any concealment run down her cheeks.

'Oh, madame . . .' she stammers, 'what is it . . .? Don't cry . . .'

Scarcely realizing what she does, she loosens the clenched, cold fingers, chilled by their prolonged contact with the metal lattice, and leads the other away from the window. The fair-haired woman submits passively, like a child, without words: too violent or too painful emotion, too long endured, seems to have deprived her of all vitality. She might be a mechanical figure but for the tears which continue their soundless rain, leaving dark spots where they fall on the purplish silk. Suddenly she stumbles over the hem of the long gown and would fall were it not for the strong young arms which support her on to the edge of the bed. This pathetic loss of dignity in one so remote, so perfect, is altogether too much for the peasant girl, already emotionalized by the sight of those incongruous tears.

Forgetting their different social status, forgetting the possibility of observation, forgetting even her work, she embraces this unhappy being as she would embrace a hurt child in her native village, murmuring inarticulate sounds of comfort. The other, who for so long has remained obdurate, confronting her equals with a disdainful, unchanging face, can allow herself to relax a little in such an uncouth clasp. It is as though she found solace in the sub-human sympathy, the mute caresses of an affectionate dog.

'Why are you being kind to me . . .? What are you saying? What language is that?' she asks at length, vague, out of her unreal world.

'It is Romansh, madame; I come from the Grisons,' the girl answers in French. The moment is slipping away, she already begins to feel a trifle awkward, incipiently aware of herself. Yet she still encircles the thin shoulders with both arms, reluctant to withdraw her support. 'Don't cry,' she says once again. 'Don't be so unhappy. It's not really bad here ... And you'll go away soon — back to your home. Can't you think of it as a little holiday?'

'I'm frightened ... quite alone ... and so far from everything,' the other replies in a whisper, tasting the tears on her mouth. She is still as if in a dream, unconscious of the inappropriate situation.

The maid, who understands nostalgia only too well, searches her brain for some consolation.

'But it's so comfortable here, madame!' she exclaims; 'and the food ...! Yesterday I brought you asparagus for lunch, and today there will be strawberries — I know because I saw the men picking them. And look — the mist is breaking! The sun will shine soon.'

Just at this moment she hears someone calling her name in the passage; it is one of the other work girls who have been sent to find out why she is being so slow over the rooms this morning.

'Yes, yes — at once — I am coming!' she cries out. She stands upright immediately; but then bends down and impulsively plants a warm peasant's kiss on the wet cheek before she crosses the room in a clumsy rush and vanishes into the corridor.

The other woman sits on in the same position, alone. Her tears have almost ceased falling: and now, for the first time in many days, there appears on her face the difficult inception of a smile.

ASYLUM PIECE

VII

A CHARMING eighteenth-century house stands just at the edge of the lake. It is really a small chateau with turrets which give it a sophisticated, frivolous, dashing air, well suited to the residence of the mistress of some distinguished personage, as which it was originally designed. The building is in an excellent state of repair, the flowering magnolia on its facade has been skillfully trained and pruned, everything indicates an appreciative and careful proprietor. Only a very sensitive observer might notice about the place an almost indescribable air, not exactly forlorn, but deprived of something, lacking the touch of individual affection, like a child brought up in an efficient institution instead of a home. There is an indefinable impersonal look about the rooms visible through the windows which are all wide open to the hot summer afternoon.

A number of people are having tea on the lawn between the house and the lake. They sit in groups round tables set in the shade of lime trees and tall acacias. Two or three women among them seem to be acting as hostesses, encouraging conversation which tends to flag and, even under their stimulus, has an oddly spasmodic character.

Marcel is the center of his particular group. For several minutes he has been talkative, amusing, gay, with a smile that comes and goes easily on his wide, flexible mouth. The vigilant hostess looks with approval upon this young man opposite her, dressed in white flannels, who is entertaining the table so well. Suddenly he observes her appreciative glance, his smile changes, loses its rather winning spontaneity, and becomes cynical, sardonic.

'Well, I've been a good boy long enough,' he thinks to himself: 'it's someone else's turn now.'

He looks at his watch, rises with a polite excuse, and picks up a racket that has been lying on the grass near his chair. It is time for him to go to his game of tennis.

The court where he is supposed to be playing is

higher up the hill, near the main building of the clinic to which all this property belongs. Swinging his racket, Marcel saunters round the elegant little château that now houses guests so different from its original occupant. With the animation gone from his face one sees that he is not so young as he seemed at the tea table; he is at least thirty — perhaps a few years older. A trace of gray has already appeared at the sides of his dark hair, there are lines in his expressive face, his eyes have a slightly strained look, a slightly overemotional brightness.

Alone on the far side of the château his steps become slower and slower until he finally stops altogether. The strokes of the stable clock sound like five languid birds floating on the warm air. He must hurry if he is not to be late for his game. He knows he ought to walk quickly up the hill, but instead he stands motionless, with drooping shoulders, the racket dangling limp from his hand. He is suffering the reaction from his recent display of sociability and vivaciousness. An expression that is at the same time bitter and mournful overshadows his face, he feels lonely, resentful, depressed. The remainder of the day stretches before him in a dreary vista of boredom, like a dull newspaper that he has already read through many times. He thinks with distaste, with irritation, of the tennis and of his partner, the red-haired American girl who sulks whenever they lose a game. She will be waiting for him now up there on the court, beginning to get bad tempered because he is five minutes late.

'Confound them all! Why should I play when I don't feel like it?' he mutters under his breath. And suddenly he turns his back on the path leading up the hill and walks down towards the lake again, passing this time round the opposite side of the château, so that he emerges on a part of the lawn some distance away from the groups at the tea tables. Although he walks quickly he has no object in view, but is merely expressing an instinctive rebellion against the boring tennis, the detestable American girl.

The low wall bordering the lake pulls him up short. He pauses irresolute, with a sense of frustration, not knowing what to do next. Finally he sits down on the warm stone wall, letting his legs hang over the water. A clump of bushes conceals him from the distant people, not one of whom seems to have noticed his presence. This makes him feel isolated, a sensation not at all pleasing to his nature, but one from which he nevertheless derives a certain masochistic satisfaction just now. For some seconds he gazes idly into the shallow, transparent, almost stagnant water through which shoals of tiny fish are busily moving. Although the water is clear it has a tepid, stale look; all sorts of unappetizing scraps of refuse have collected on the stony bed of the lake. A black, thin shape like a miniature eel comes wriggling through the shallows towards the stones at the edge; it is a leech. With a suppressed ex-clamation of disgust Marcel looks in another direction.

His glance now falls on a rowing boat moored a few yards away. Usually the boat is padlocked to an iron ring in the wall, but now it is only loosely secured by a knotted rope. He vaguely remembers seeing the gym mistress unfasten the padlock while he was sitting at tea. Perhaps some of the patients are going out for a row. Well, that does not interest him any more than the tennis. He raises his wide, bright, unstable eyes and sees, straight across the smooth water, the French coast with its mountains and its lower hills crested with countless poplars.

Immediately a new thought sequence springs to activity in his brain. 'It's high time I went home. I ought to get back to work or I shall be losing all my connections. A barrister can't afford to take such long holidays, even if he has a rich wife —' He tries to reckon up how many months he has spent in the clinic, but somehow the calculation eludes him, and this inability to concentrate on a simple question of dates increases his general discontent. 'All the days are alike in this wretched place — One quite loses count of time,' he thinks angrily. And then: 'Why are they still keeping me here? I'm quite well — it's not as if there ever was much wrong with me. I'd been overworking — I only needed a rest. Now I'm perfectly fit, and yet they still keep me hanging about — wasting my time.' He scowls as he thinks of the doctors, of the evasive replies they give him when he suggests fixing a day for his departure. 'Of course, it's just a money-making concern: they're all a lot of sharks trying to make as much out of us as they can.'

The mental picture of his wife now passes before him, a handsome young woman, rather plump, and beautifully dressed in black with pearls round her throat: it is she who is paying for him to stay at the clinic. An atrocious suspicion that often crosses his mind causes him to pick up a stone and hurl it viciously into the lake, startling the small fish out of their ceaseless voyaging. 'No, it's simply not possible — no one could be so wicked, so unscrupulous. I musn't allow myself to imagine such terrible things.'

All the same, he can no longer remain quietly sitting on the wall, but jumps up and takes a few restless paces in the direction of the rowing boat, above which he stands, tapping his foot against the iron ring in which the mooring rope is attached.

'If only I could be certain what's going on at home. If only I could get back,' he says to himself, now for the first time admitting in his own mind that there exists some obstacle to his departure. A fantasy of leave-taking next occupies him: he imagines himself packing his luggage, going up to the chief doctor and demanding his money, his passport, booking a sleeper on the Paris train. 'Yes, I'll do it,' he says aloud, twice, first with enthusiasm, then with dwindling conviction. But he does not move to put the plan into practice: something which he cannot, dare not, acknowledge, forbids him to make the attempt.

Instead, he begins to think nostalgically of his old life, the gaiety of the city, of his work, and of his friends who will be so pleased to see him again. He looks across the lake at the mountains of Savoie, his own country: and it seems to him that only this negligible strip of water, which looks as smoothly solid as if one could walk over it, divides him from the fulfillment of his desires.

A sudden idea comes to him, and it is curious to observe the rapid change in his face which now all at once assumes a mischievous, crafty expression. He glances at the people sitting rather more than the width of the château away. Enervated by the hot afternoon, not a soul seems to have moved, not a soul is paying any attention to him. He stoops down and with hurried movements unfastens the knotted rope: then springs into the boat and hastily rows off. A few strong pulls carry him round a small promontory, out of sight of the château grounds. Smiling, with an almost roguish look, he rows on with powerful, regular strokes.

Soon he is far out from the land, alone in his boat in the midst of the practically colorless expanse of smooth water. About half a dozen other small boats are scattered over the lake. They are far away from him, but he is glad of their presence which means that his own boat will be less conspicuous from the shore. There is no breeze, it is very hot, the air shimmers with heat. Sweat rolls down Marcel's face, but he does not mind; still smiling his roguish smile, he wipes the sweat out of his eyes and rows on. His bare, brown, muscular arms swing to an indefatigable rhythm. This man who would not find energy for a game of tennis is now quite happy toiling in the blind watery glare, gratified by his own strength.

It is farther than he expected across the lake, but before very long the French coast is appreciably nearer, he can distinguish the windows of houses, then human figures, then dogs and chickens moving about. He rows parallel with the shore for a little way seeking a secluded landing place: he has the idea that it might be wiser not to land in a village where he could be questioned immediately. He has not formulated any plan of action as yet. So far, he has been occupied solely with the physical effort and with the elation he feels at his own enterprise.

Now he has found just the place to land, a curved beach like a diminutive bay, out of sight of all dwellings, with green grass banks rising steeply above. He brings the boat close to the shore but makes no attempt to disembark. He sits still, with the oars trailing in the water and the sweat slowly drying on his face which now begins to acquire a look of uncertainty. Why does he hesitate? All he has to do is to ground the boat, to jump out and climb up the bank into his own land. True, he has no passport and only a few coins of trifling value in his pockets: but still, he will be free, safe, among his own countrymen. He has only to explain his position to someone in authority and all will arrange itself satisfactorily: a telephone call will be put through to Paris, his railway fare will be advanced to him, he will be at home in the morning.

Yes, it all seems so simple, and yet he can't bring himself to get out of the boat. What is it that prevents him from stepping ashore? What is it that tells him that it is safer not to think, safer to remain vague, to realize nothing? Dimly, through a haze of unreality, he envisages the gendarmes, the questions, the significant looks. But all these things are far off, unimminent, cloudy. Much better not to think about them, much better not to put things to the test, much better not to risk having realization forced upon one.

All the archness, the volatileness, has vanished with the smile from his face. He now looks much older, worn and dejected. The spirit has quite gone out of him. He feels very tired. Slowly, wearily, with a deep sigh, his eyes empty and downcast, he takes hold of the oars and begins the laborious passage back to the other shore.

ASYLUM PIECE

VIII

IN the clinic, as in heaven, there are many mansions. The worst cases, and those requiring the most supervision, are lodged in a house called 'La Pinède' which stands some distance away from the main building. Metal scrolls guard the windows of this house and there is only one outer door that is always kept locked. An attendant is constantly on duty to unfasten and relock the door each time anyone passes through.

The attendant sits in a little room, white and bare as a nun's cell, just to the left of the door. This morning quite a young girl is on duty there. She is bright and pleasant looking in her superlatively clean overall, she has put a bunch of flowers on the table where she sits with her English grammar, her notebook and pencil. She is industrious, she means to get on in the world, and she studies her book with concentration. Nevertheless, she finds time to glance occasionally at the little bunch of wild cyclamen which she picked yesterday in the forest with a young man in whom she is interested. Everything about her is normal, cheerful, serene. It is difficult to associate the contented girl with the hidden unhappiness that surrounds her under this roof.

She hears footsteps approaching and goes out into the hall.

A middle-aged English lady is waiting for the door to be opened. She is rather tall, rather large, and wears a mauve knitted dress that clings to her solid figure. Her faded hair is encircled with a bandeau of brown tulle which gives her an air that somehow contrives to be both impressive and slightly comic. She has the intensely respectable, intensely reserved look so characteristic of a certain old-fashioned type of Englishwoman abroad. One would expect to find her in a *pension* at Mentone, making tea in her bedroom over a spirit lamp, or perhaps painting precise little watercolors with a good deal of ultramarine. Today is one of her good days. There is nothing at all in her appearance to suggest the moods of suicidal depression which are the cause of her presence at 'La Pinède.'

'Good morning, Miss Swanson,' says the smiling attendant in careful English, as she unlocks the door.

Miss Swanson answers and smiles in her remote way and goes out into the sun. After the shadows indoors the bright light is like a blow and she stops to put on the dark spectacles that she carries about in her bag. In front of her, in the middle of the asphalted private road, is a round bed full of succulent looking cannas; behind, to the right and left, is the pinewood from which the house takes its name. When she has adjusted her glasses Miss Swanson puts up a linen sunshade lined with green and walks slowly along the middle of the roadway that leads both to the main building and to the workroom for which she is bound.

As she goes, she has, from some distance away, a clear view of what is happening ahead. From time to time, at irregular intervals, singly or in small groups, figures emerge from the white balconied house and walk towards the atelier. All of them, in passing, pause for a few seconds beside a small, solitary girlish form under a clump of trees: the distant girl in her gay summer frock seems to have some piece of news which she is imparting to each one in turn.

The woman with the sunshade watches this procedure intently, screwing up her eyes behind their dark screens. The contraction of her eyes seems to indicate anxiety or disapproval — perhaps both. She begins to walk faster.

Soon she comes within speaking distance of the girl who is now alone, half sitting on an iron table under the trees. She is so small boned and slight, her body is so immature looking, that at a first glance one would take her for a child of about fifteen. It is hard to believe that she is actually a married woman when she calls out to her friend:

'My husband's come! He's with the doctors now. As soon as he's finished with them he's going to take me out for the day.' She jumps up and siezes Miss Swanson's arm impulsively, shaking back her soft, fluffy hair and exclaiming: 'I told you he'd come, didn't I? You didn't believe me, but you see I was right all the time!' She tilts her head and laughs rather aimlessly, glancing up at the elder woman who, for her part, looks down gravely into the pretty, childish, undisciplined face which seems to lack some coordination with its receding chin, its large, slightly prominent blue eyes.

'How nice for you, Freda,' she says, noncommittal.

The lukewarm tone disappoints the other who pouts and moves a few petulant steps away, putting a space between the two of them.

'You don't sound a bit pleased,' she complains in an aggrieved tone.

Miss Swanson advances and pats her on the shoulder.

'Gracious, how thin you are, child!' she mutters to herself, feeling the bones under their inadequate coverings of silk and flesh. A thwarted maternal instinct in her has fastened upon this girl, her compatriot, who, like herself, is an exile, almost a prisoner, in this unhappy place. She feels possessive, protective, towards Freda; jealous of anyone who might come between them. 'Of course I'm pleased that you're happy,' she goes on. 'But I'm afraid for you — that things will be worse for you afterwards — that you'll feel lonelier than ever when your husband has gone.'

'But he's not going!' cries Freda triumphantly. 'He's going to stay at the hotel by the lake.'

'All the same, he'll have to go back to England sometime.'

'Then he'll take me with him — I'll persuade him — you'll see. I'm quite well now, anyhow.'

The childish face is all smiles and Miss Swanson has not got the heart to refrain from smiling back in return. But she says nothing, and as it happens she is spared the necessity for words, because at that moment Mr. Rushwood comes out on to the steps of the clinic. He is very much older than his wife — perhaps more than twice her age — the last man in the world one would expect her to marry, for his face is serious, repressive, almost stern, under his gray hair. He approaches stiffly in the sunshine, walking with rather a wooden gait on account of an old war wound in the right leg. Freda introduces her friend, and he smiles like a schoolmaster, without warmth. His voice, too, is the voice of a master or of a clergyman, authoritative and cool.

'Well, what did the doctors say? Did they tell you how good I've been?' Freda is asking, clinging on to his arm and beaming at him.

But he, without answering the question, advises her to go and fetch her hat and bag as the car will arrive in a moment.

She runs off, like a docile child, and the elders are left together in the shade of the trees. Neither speaks. Mr. Rushwood stands stiffly by the table with an expressionless face. He is preoccupied; and a little embarrassed, too, at being left alone with this stranger who, though she looks quite conventional, may at any moment display some disturbing eccentricity. Miss Swanson surveys him with eyes that, in spite of everything, are shrewd enough behind the concealing black lenses. She does not seem to find reassurance in his aspect. Presently she puts up the sunshade which she has folded during the conversation with Freda, and starts to move off. But then a sudden impulse, very rare in her restrained spinster's heart, makes her turn back and address the uncompromising man.

'Mr Rushwood, will you allow me to say something which I really have no right to say? You may quite well tell me that your wife's future is no business of mine, and I can only answer that nothing but my very genuine affection for her would induce me to interfere in matters which do not concern me. During the last few weeks I have come to know Freda very well, she has confided in me, and I understand her character. Perhaps, if you will forgive my saying so, I understand her even better than you do. Of course I don't know what plans you have made for her, but, Mr. Rushwood, I do beg you most earnestly to consider very carefully whether this is the right place for her — whether it would not be better to take her away from an environment where she is lonely and sad and where she is bound to see and hear things which would be shocking to any young girl and must be especially so to one so sensitive and highly-strung as she is.

If you leave her here when you go I am really afraid of what may happen to her — I am really afraid she will break her heart.'

It is the proof of Miss Swanson's love that she is able to urge a course of action so contrary to her own wishes, for without Freda her existence at the clinic would loose its last shred of value.

The visitor has been growing slowly more uncomfortable during her long speech which, though spoken in a perfectly quiet voice, strikes him as being charged with dangerous emotion. For the first time he displays some sign of feeling, as, with a look half irritable, half apprehensive, he glances about as if in search of assistance. 'This is insupportable!' he thinks indignantly: 'why doesn't someone come and take the woman away?' But there is nobody at all in sight and he is obliged to make a reply.

'My dear madam, even though you don't credit me with any understanding of my wife, you must at least allow the doctors' opinion —' he is beginning coldly, when two things occur simultaneously to rescue him from further embarrassment: a car sweeps round the bend of the private road and Freda rushes through the door of the clinic and comes running down the steps.

With only the briefest of salutes to his companion Rushwood goes across to the car where the girl is already sitting. Miss Swanson slowly waves her hand in response to Freda's fluttering handkerchief. She watches the car out of sight and then walks in a dispirited way towards the workshop and the lamp-shade upon which she is stenciling a floral design. She knows that the day will pass drearily for her now.

For Freda, on the contrary, the hours fly like happy birds. Like a child just back from boarding-school for the holidays she wants to see everything, to do everything at once. The small lakeside town is a heaven to her; she darts in and out of shops, eating pastries and chocolates, buying absurd trifles, chattering all the while to her husband, whose attitude is more like that of a father, at the same time indulgent, distrait, and somewhat im-patient. At lunch on the terrace of the hotel he can no longer restrain his impatience but sharply re-proves the girl for her indecorous behavior which, he fancies, is attracting the attention of the people around. Freda is cast-down and subdued for a few moments, but she soon forgets the rebuke and laughs and talks as irrepressibly as before.

The husband is rapidly coming to an end of his store of indulgence. The fact that the waiters obviously take Freda for his daughter and address her as 'madamoiselle' adds to his annoyance. He feels tired and worried, his leg is beginning to hurt him, he can no longer see anything but the faults in Freda's conduct. Finally he suggests a trip on the lake. It seems to him that her childish irresponsibility and exuberance will be less noticeable on the steamer.

From the man's point of view the afternoon is more satisfactory than the morning. To be sure, his wife is excited by the boat to begin with; she runs from one side to the other, leaning eagerly over the rail at the landing stages to watch the people embark, and throwing bread to the gulls which mysteriously, so far from any sea, follow the steamer like white shadows. But towards the end of the trip she becomes quieter, sitting beside him on the wooden bench, her hand affectionately curled round his fingers. He spreads his coat over their knees so that no one shall see that she is holding his hand.

At dinner her febrile animation returns. The evening is chilly, instead of eating on the terrace they are now in the long dining room. Her large, bright, prominent eyes dart mischievously from table to table, her indefatigable voice pours out its treble comments upon the diners. Once more Rushwood is forced to reprove her.

'Really, Freda, you are acting like a bad-mannered schoolgirl. Can't you realize that it's not amusing but merely rude to make personal remarks?'

'But they don't understand what we're saying —'

The note of almost unbearable irritation sounding through the deliberately calm tone in which he has just spoken penetrates her child's heart like a cruel needle of ice. Her face falls grotesquely, her mouth trembles, tears — the sudden, despairing tears of a hurt child — fill her eyes to the brim.

'All right, all right — there's nothing to cry about,' he says hastily, dreading a public scene.

Fortunately, the waiter creates a diversion by bringing a dish of ice cream. Rushwood rests his chin on his hands and gazes across the small table at the girl who is now intent on the pink frozen substance upon her plate. Bitterness fills his being. Although his nature is cold and inflexible he is not a particularly unkind man, he wishes no ill to his wife; it is only that he can feel no sympathy, no toleration for her: his bitterness is directed against fate that has used him so evilly. He cannot understand why this dispropor-tionate punishment should be inflicted upon him because he was once infatuated by a pretty face. 'But who could have guessed it would turn out like this?' he thinks wearily. He is glad that the meal is over, that the long, trying day has almost come to an end, that it is time to return his charge to the doctors' care.

The car is waiting for them outside the hotel. He is profoundly relieved because Freda raises no objection to going back to the clinic. In his gratitude he feels more warmly towards her than he has done all day long: in the dusky seclusion of the car he touches her hand.

'You never showed me your room in the hotel,'

she exclaims suddenly, as they start to climb the steep, curving road from the lake.

It has come now, the dangerous moment, the moment he dreads. But the lights of the clinic are in sight; he is saved.

'I'm afraid I shan't be staying,' he says evenly. 'I have to get back to the office. It's not easy for me to get away even for a few days just now.'

There is dead silence inside the car. Even he, unimaginative and withdrawn as he is, feels the burden of silence. 'Why doesn't she say something?' he wonders, peering at the averted whiteness that is her face. The car takes the final bend sharply and her body is thrown against his.

Suddenly she grasps his shoulders with both hands; he is surprised at the strength of her fingers, he feels her pointed fingers nipping into his flesh through the jacket and shirt.

'You can't leave me here . . . You must take me back with you!' she cries shrilly, against his chest.

'Now, Freda, do try and be reasonable. You know perfectly well that I can't take you — that the doctors say you must stay here for the present.'

He tries to disengage her fingers; but he cannot capture her hands which, like desperate sparrows, are beating all about him, clawing at his sleeve, his lapels, his tie, even his face. He can do nothing except dumbly defend himself against those clawing, beating hands, his ears deafened and appalled by the broken treble that fills the interior of the closed car with ceaseless, inarticulate lamentation.

They have come now to the entrance of the clinic. The chauffeur opens the car door and looks inside, then quickly shuts the door again with a muttered, 'One moment, monsieur.' He does not seem at all taken aback by what he sees in the car; probably he is quite used to such happenings. Almost at once he is back again with two nurses. 'If you will get out here, monsieur — that will be best,' he says to the confused husband, efficient and matter-of-fact.

The nurses prepare to restrain Freda in case she tries to prevent this move. But she, as if automatically giving up hope at the sight of authority, has already ceased all protest, all aggression, and is huddled unresistingly in the corner, limp as a doll, with tears running down her cheeks.

189

Mr. Rushwood steps out, with mechanical movements tidying his disordered attire. The car quickly
drives on.

'Silly little thing!' one of the nurses says, quite
kindly, to the sobbing girl. 'This will mean 'La
Pinède' for you.'

They reach the house in the pinewood and wait for
the door to be opened. The women in white
support Freda who is weeping and trembling so
violently that she can scarcely stand. A light is
switched on over the door revealing her face
glistening all over with tears like the face of a
person just emerging from water. The chauffeur
watches with an impartial air as the three enter and
the door is locked after them.

In the hall, which is dimly lit, someone moves
out of the shadows and approaches the group. It is
Miss Swanson who has waited a long time patiently
for this moment. Dressed now in a blue knitted
dress of exactly the same style as the mauve one
which she wore earlier in the day, she comes up to
the girl and, ignoring the nurses entirely, enfolds
her in a compassionate and triumphant embrace.

The End in Sight

THE END IN SIGHT

IT is three days since I received the official notification of my sentence; three days that have passed like shadows, like dreams.

The letter came through the post in the ordinary way and arrived by the late afternoon delivery. Curiously enough, I was feeling more cheerful that afternoon than I had felt for a long time. The sun was shining, it was a lovely, calm day, one of those premature spring days which sometimes come to encourage us towards the end of a long, hard winter. The beautiful weather made me decide to go out; it really seemed shameful to stay shut up indoors with one's worries when the outside world was full of sunshine and life. I went across the fields towards the wood on the hill. This has always been a favorite walk of mine, and as I went I was astonished to think how long it was since I had last been that way and how my habits had changed, how I myself had altered, since the case started againt me.

The colors of the landscape were as if washed

pure and true in the transparent, windless light, vivid new sproutings like chilly flames appeared here and there in the hedges, the boughs of the trees were clouded with purplish buds. From the old yew on the hillside, disturbed by my footsteps, emerged with their strangely silent, sure flight the two brown owls which I watched like old friends. Walking back to the house I made a resolution to go out more in future, not to stay indoors aimlessly brooding, but to make the most of the natural world and to identify myself with non-human things, since they at least held no threat over me.

Oh, if only I'd known what I should find when I went inside my door! But no premonition warned me of what was coming, on the contrary; as I've said, I felt more optimistic than I've felt since goodness knows when. I remember that as I crossed the garden from the field gate I was thinking about a man named David P. whom I had met some time previously, a man who was in the same position as I was, waiting to hear the result of his case, and whose tranquil, courageous bearing under conditions of almost   intolerable   strain   had   aroused   my admiration. 'How do you manage to keep so calm all the time?' I has asked him, half believing that he must be in possession of some inside information, or perhaps had influence in official quarters. And I had remarked, too, on the fact that he alone of all the accused people I had ever met, wore an unanxious, almost happy expression.

'Oh well, one doesn't gain anything by worrying, does one?' he had answered me. 'You may be sure that all the worrying in the world isn't going to affect the final issue for us. In fact, I'm inclined to believe that the less we think about our cases the better: if one has confidence in one's advisor one can safely leave everything to him. As for looking cheerful, there's still a lot left in life that we can enjoy. The great secret, in my opinion, is to concentrate on the things which can't be taken away from one — the past, for instance, and trees, and poetry . . .' Of course, I had often thought of this conversation before, but only now — and how ironic that realization should have come just then! — did I seem to realize the personal application of what David had said.

With these thoughts occupying my mind I went into the house. The afternoon post had come and the letters were still lying on the floor where they had fallen when the postman pushed them through the slit in the door. I bent down to pick them up. At first there seemed to be nothing of interest; only a circular and one or two bills or receipts. But then, half hidden by a bulb catalogue, I saw the pale blue, official envelope, I felt the familiar stiffness of the paper in my hand, and my heart quickened its beat.

Right up to that moment I had no suspicion of what the letter contained. From time to time, ever since my case started, these pale blue documents have descended upon me, sometimes with a form to be filled in, sometimes with an ambiguous message or with an extract from some incomprehensible blue book, and I, unsuspectingly, took this for another communication of the same kind. Even when I had torn open the envelope and read through the paper enclosed I failed at the start to take in the meaning of the words.

'It can't be true — someone's playing a joke on me,' I thought, as the import of the sentences slowly penetrated my mind. 'Surely this isn't how it's done — through the post — in this casual way —? Surely they'd at least send somebody — a messenger —' But then a curious vibration, like running water, seemed to flow over the walls, I saw the walls leaning nearer, as if watchfully, I knew very well that the letter was not a trick; and I was glad that I was alone in the hall with only the walls watching to see my face.

That was what happened three days ago. Since then time has passed in an unreal flux. Perhaps today, perhaps tomorrow, the final blow will fall: I know that I have, at the most, another week or ten days. What is the correct behavior for a condemned person? — the authorities have never sent me a pamphlet containing that information! Sometimes I feel almost relieved to think that it is all over, that the suspense is finished at last. At other times it seems to me that I am quite incapable of realizing that this is the end. I look at the elm trees over which the thickening buds have flung a soft purple bloom, and it seems incredible that I shall not even see the leaves as big as the ears of mice.

No, no — it's simply absurd — it can't be true . . .
It's somebody else who has received the fatal pale
blue notification — perhaps David P.: he would
know how to behave in such circumstances; he would
bear philosophically and with fortitude the sentence
which I am not brave enough even to contemplate.

I am constantly aware of the heart beating inside
my breast, strongly and resolutely pumping the
blood through my veins. Once I read somewhere
that when the blood is thin it wants to return
whence it came. But my blood is not thin, my blood
does not want to fall back. Unbearable reluctance of
the blood that will not fall! How many, dying on the
scaffold, must have suffered this unspeakable
punishment, not to be justified by any penal code.

Yesterday afternoon I lay down on the couch in
my living room. I had scarcely slept at all the
previous night and felt I must rest a little. But I had
hardly put my head on the cushions when a voice
seemed to shout in my ear: 'What, are you going
to waste an hour with your eyes closed when perhaps
this is their last hour for seeing anything?'

I jumped up, like a demented person, like

someone driven by furies, I hurried through the rooms of the house, hurried into the garden and into the fields, straining my eyes to appreciate every detail, straining to store up within my brain the images of all these things which are so soon to be hidden from me forever. Later on, quite exhasuted, I went into the inn for a drink; but no sooner was the glass in my hand than I felt an impulse to throw it away, unwilling to dim even with a single drop of alcohol the sharp vision of what might be the last scene upon which I should ever look.

People were there whom I knew. They laughed and spoke together about the coming summer and what they would do in the long summer days. How could I stay and listen to their talk, knowing that while they are carrying out the plans made so carelessly I shall be far away from every activity? And how can I stay at home, either, answering the questions of the gardener about seeds for the summer, and hearing the chatter of my little girl who knows nothing of what is happening to me, and who also talks of the future, of the summer, and of what we will do together?

The hours pass, some slowly, some like flashes of light, but each one leading me inexorably nearer to the end. Incredulous, I watch the hours pass without bringing any reprieve. 'Isn't anyone going to do anything, then?' I want to cry out. 'Isn't anything going to happen to save me? They can't let me be destroyed like this. A message must come to say it was all a mistake. Somebody must do something.'

But no one around me even knows what is going on. Only the dog seems to sense that all is not well with me. And when, just now, unable to bear my sufferings any longer in silence, I whispered to him, 'Oh, Tige, I'll soon have to leave you — this dreadful thing is really going to happen to me — nothing will save me now,' I saw a dimness like tears in his lustrous brown eyes.

There is no End

THERE IS NO END

'WHITHER shall I go from thy spirit?
Whither shall I flee from thy presence?
If I ascend into heaven thou art there.
If I make my bed in hell, behold, thou art there.
If I take the wings of the morning, even there
    thy hand shall lead me.'

I can't think properly these days, I find it difficult
to remember, but I suppose those words were
written about Jehovah, though they apply just as
well to my enemy — if that is what I should call
him.

'If I make my bed in hell, behold, thou art there.'
That particular phrase rings in my brain with a horrid
aptness: for certainty I have made my bed in hell and
certainly he is here with me. He is near all the time although I do not see him. Only sometimes, very early
in the morning before it has got light, I seem to catch
a glimpse of a half-familiar face peering in at the
window; but it is always snatched away so quickly

that I have no time to recognize it. And just once, one evening, the door of my room was suddenly opened a little way and somebody glanced in through the crack, glanced in, and then passed hurriedly out of sight down the corridor. Perhaps that was he.

Why does he keep his eye on me like this now that he has accomplished his purpose and brought about my destruction? It can't be to make sure that I don't escape; oh, no, there's no possibility of that, he need not have the slightest fear. Is it just to gloat over my ruin? But no, I don't think that's the reason, either, for if that were so he would come more often and at times more humiliating to me when I am in the deepest despair.

Somehow I have the impression from those vague glimpses I have caught of his face that it wears a look that is not vindictive, but kindred, almost as though he were related closely to me by some similarity of brain or blood. And of late the idea has come to me — fantastic enough, I admit — that possibly after all he is not my personal enemy, but a sort of projection of myself, an identification of myself with the cruelty and destructiveness of the world. On a planet where there is so much natural conflict may there not very well exist in certain individuals an overwhelming affinity with frustration and death? And may this not result in an actual materialization, a sort of eidolon moving about the world?

I have thought a lot about such matters of late, sitting here and looking out of the window. For, strangely enough, there are windows without bars in this place and doors which are not even locked. Apparently there is nothing to prevent me from walking out whenever I feel inclined. Yet though there is no visible barrier I know only too well that I am surrounded by unseen and impassable walls which tower into the highest domes of the zenith and sink many miles below the surface of the earth.

So it has come upon me, the doom too long awaited, the end without end, the bannerless triumph of the enemy who, after all, appears to be close as a brother. Already it seems to me that I have spent a lifetime in this narrow room whose walls will continue to regard me with secrecy through innumerable lifetimes to come. Is it life, then, or death, stretching like an uncolored stream behind and in front of me? There is no love here, nor hate, nor any point where feeling accumulates. In this nameless place nothing appears animate, nothing is close, nothing is real; I am pursued by the remembered scent of dust sprinkled with summer rain.

Outside my window there is a garden where nobody ever walks: a garden without seasons, for the trees are all evergreens. At certain times of the day I can hear the clatter of footsteps on the concrete covered ways which intersect the lawns, but the garden is always deserted, set for the casual appreciation of strangers, or else for the remote and solitary contemplation of eyes defeated like mine. In this impersonal garden, all neatness and vacancy, there is no arbor where friends could linger, but only concrete paths along which people walk hurriedly, inattentive to the singing of birds.

BUDIMIR MEMORIAL LIBRARY

Dec 16/80

W I T H D R A W N
FROM THE COLLECTION OF
WINDSOR PUBLIC LIBRARY

BECAUSE OF SPECIAL DEMAND
THIS ITEM MAY BE KEPT ONLY
7 DAYS